SHAROO'S
GREAT DECISION

ALSO BY W.W. ROWE

SHAROO'S
GREAT DECISION

W.W. ROWE
Benjamin Slatoff-Burke, Illustrator

LARSON PUBLICATIONS
BURDETT, NEW YORK

ISBN-10: 1-936012-98-7
ISBN-13: 978-1-936012-98-5

Library of Congress Control Number: 2023937542

Publisher's Cataloging-In-Publication Data
(Provided by Cassidy Cataloguing Services, Inc.)

Names:	Rowe, William Woodin, author.	Slatoff-Burke, Benjamin, illustrator.	Rowe, William Woodin. Eedoo trilogy.
Title:	Sharoo's great decision / W.W. Rowe ; Benjamin Slatoff-Burke, illustrator.
Description:	Burdett, New York : Larson Publications, [2023]	A sequel to the Eedoo trilogy.	Interest age level: 12 and up.	Summary: This fifth and final, culminating episode of Rowe's ... Sharoo adventures spans sixty years--from Sharoo's teen years and marriage with Clyde as rulers of Broan, through surviving many droll Bart jokes, supporting clever new technology, defending Plash from two sinister breeches of its protective portals, having two children, and aging into their end years. Sharoo glimpses the afterlife, learns of her past incarnations, and what can come next if she chooses.--Publisher.
Identifiers:	ISBN: 978-1-936012-98-5 (paperback)	LCCN: 2023937542
Subjects:	LCSH: Imaginary places--Juvenile fiction.	Heroes--Juvenile fiction.	Kings and rulers-- Juvenile fiction.	Future life--Juvenile fiction.	CYAC: Imaginary places--Fiction.	Heroes-- Fiction.	Kings, queens, rulers, etc.--Fiction.	Future life--Fiction.	LCGFT: Fantasy fiction.	BISAC: YOUNG ADULT FICTION / Fantasy / Wizards & Witches.	JUVENILE FICTION / Fantasy & Magic.	JUVENILE FICTION / Girls & Women.
Classification:	LCC: PZ7.R7953 Sh 2023	DDC: [Fic]--dc23

Published by Larson Publications
4936 NYS Route 414
Burdett, New York 14818 USA

https://www.larsonpublications.com
32 31 30 29 28 27 26 25 24 23
10 9 8 7 6 5 4 3 2 1

Life is a preparation for death, just as
death is a preparation for re-entry.

—Paul Brunton

Dedication

This fifth and final Sharoo story, spanning sixty years and offering a presumptuous glimpse of the afterlife, is dedicated to Paul Brunton, my wife Eleanor, and our grandson August. And to my deceased brother Bill, who believed in rebirth and playfully mused about having a gravestone that said: "Now he knows."

Acknowledgments

Many thanks to my wife Eleanor and Sylvia Somerville for their helpful suggestions. Also to Amy and Paul Cash, for their essential insights, wordings, and wisdom. Of course, any goofs or gaffes are my own.

ONE

Plash, you may recall, is a small, exotic planet in a parallel universe.

Many years ago, the Wizard Wombler used his awesome magic to create the weird weather of Plash—from purple rain that tastes like grape soda to huge, floppy snowflakes. He also established five interdimensional portals.

The country of Broan, on Plash, boasts a Simon Says School. Giggling laffodils dot the countryside. In the forests, deadly boa vines lurk. Hanging from trees, these green reptilic plants swing slowly toward their careless prey . . . and lunge. Hunters sometimes find clean white skeletons beneath them.

After thirteen-year-old Sharoo was elected Queen of Broan, she made her boyfriend Clyde the King. They now rule Broan together with their Floaters.

What is a Floater? An invisible, eternal presence, like a guardian angel, only more. Little Broanian children are naturally "in tune" with their Floaters. Ridiculed by scornful adults, they stop believing. What a pity! Their Floaters could have given them so much helpful guidance.

Our previous book (*Sharoo: Teen Queen*) ended by focusing on two eerie secrets.

First, Queen Sharoo hadn't told King Clyde that she utilized two magic portals to go back in spacetime and save him after he had *already* been bewitched, seduced, and murdered.

Second, the old seer Mrs. Zaura hadn't told Queen Sharoo that after Wizard Wombler died, he was reborn as the girl herself!

An old Broanian saying goes: "Keep a secret, and it won't bite."

Now you can find out if these two eerie secrets were kept. And discover the nature of Sharoo's great decision.

TWO

It's a beautiful blue Oneday in Broan City, capital of Broan. A week here is ten days long.

Above the royal castle, three gray dolphin clouds swoop and slide. Are these playful, fishlike clouds alive? They were created by the Wizard Wombler long ago. Does their number, as sometimes seems to happen, suggest a significant aspect of the future?

In the Shipshape Sea, sun-dazzled waves lap the rocky shore. Standing high above the frothy rocks, the castle's gem-studded walls brightly glitter. Did Wombler cast a protective spell upon these sparkling jewels? Even by darkest night, no thief has ever dared to scale the walls and pry them loose.

In the royal bedchamber, Queen Sharoo and King Clyde languidly awake. As if choreographed, they simultaneously stretch and yawn. The monogrammed purple sheets are twisted.

"Morning, sweet." Sharoo's voice is warm and husky. Her silky yellow bangs are tangled, which Clyde loves. Sharoo's birth sign is the extremely rare Silver Dragon.

"Hi, Roo." Smiling, Clyde gives her a lengthy kiss. He has curly black hair, delicate emerald-green eyes, and light-brown skin. Clyde is a Crystal Deer.

"I'm glad the Council approved our request," he murmurs. (The King and Queen had asked for a one-time "royal dispensation," allowing them to marry sooner than at Broan's normal legal age.)

Their wedding had been a splendid affair. Sharoo, with her silky yellow hair and glorious nuptial gown, resembled a golden goddess. Clyde in his blue suit seemed to be coming truly into his own. Hordes of Broanians crowded around the bamboo temple, cheering with joy.

True, a few were skeptical. "Too extravagant!" muttered old Cyrus Finki. "A gold coin for everyone who attended!" "Too young," scowled others. But most people were filled with happiness for their young royal couple.

Now, Sharoo says, "We need to meditate."

Once again in unison, they jump from the bed, float to the floor, and shuffle to the royal suite's twin water rooms. (Plash, you may recall, is a small planet, so gravity is very weak. The people wear heavy shoes.)

Refreshed and back in the bedchamber, they sit poised on gold cushions. Prior to meditation, their first thoughts focus on their Floaters.

"Hi, Eeroo," Clyde murmurs.

"Morning, Eedoo," Sharoo faintly whispers.

No answer from either Floater, but the King and Queen can sense their presence.

"Anything we should know?" Sharoo softly asks.

This time, she receives an answer. *Dangerous aliens are likely to invade Broan.* The words sound softly inside her head. Floaters can see a variety of probable and possible futures.

Sharoo gasps. "Is there another land we don't know about, like Lollia?"

No. These invaders live on another planet.

The girl's eyes grow wide. "What . . . do they look like?"

No answer.

Lurid images float up in Sharoo's mind. Slimy monsters with tentacles. Evil creatures with sharp green teeth. "Eedoo! Are you showing me this, or is it just my imagination?"

Silence.

"Can you at least tell me what planet?" In her mind, she runs through the names of the other five planets: Vortex, Blore . . .

No answer.

At the same time, Clyde hears a warning from Eeroo: *Deadly-dangerous beings are likely to come here from another planet.*

Clyde shudders. "What beings?" he whispers. "What planet?"

Silence.

Floaters often don't reply. Even when they do, they sometimes only offer enigmatic hints. People must do things mostly by themselves.

The royal teenagers stare at each other helplessly.

"Did Eedoo tell you?" asks Clyde.

"Yes. Maybe the invaders will come from Vortex."

"No, too hot." Clyde is mentally reviewing The Sleep Song. (In Broan, parents sing it to their children: "Very peaceful, baby. Just sleep, please." This melody calms tiny kids. Later it helps them remember the names of the planets: Vortex, Plash, Blore, Justin, Saturling, and Plexo—same first letters as the song.)

"Maybe the invaders will come from Blore," says Clyde. "Those Morfers are vicious and mean."

"I don't think so," Sharoo muses. "They took off pretty fast when I made up a magic spell to scare them. What should we do?"

15

"Let's ask."

They close their eyes, tilt back their heads, and whisper. Silence.

"We don't have any idea what to do!" Sharoo pleads.

Both she and Clyde hear the same words:

For now, have a good meditation.

Anxious to comply, the royal couple meditates with quiet determination. They pray to The O.B.E. for Inspiration. (In Broan, that means The One Behind Everything. Broanians love acronyms.)

"A.S.A.P.," Sharoo thinks. "Alert, still, and poised."

In her cozy castle guest room, the witch-like seer Mrs. Zaura opens her squinty eyes. She peers upward toward the ornate, pink-and-blue-flowered ceiling. "Hello, Eebliz."

Good morning. The words echo softly in the old woman's head.

"Prithee, what may you reveal?"

No imminent problems. But a deadly menace, like the eye of a distant tynado, is forming on another planet.

"Deadly menace!"

Correct. Hostile invaders may soon come to Broan.

"And you won't say who they are, of course."

Correct.

"Well, that's a fine kettle of vipers." Mrs. Zaura frowns. "I'd better do some serious trancing today."

Already, the seer senses that there are now three warnings.

To call for morn-meal, she pulls the tasseled strip of tapestry that hangs beside her bed. Two servant boys, Awn and Auff, take turns bringing the old lady's food on silver trays.

THREE

Sharoo and Clyde enter the sunlit dining hall. Their friends Milli Potch and Bart Filo are already devouring butter-cream pancakes with zingberry syrup. Bright sunbeams sparkle on the dishes and silver.

After making Clyde King, Queen Sharoo invited Milli and Bart to move into the castle. A few clever citizens now refer to the castle, rather good-naturedly, as "The Nursery." The King and Queen, they jest, "rule Broan from high chairs."

Genuine respect is in short supply. It doesn't help that all four teenagers wear plain cotton shirts, bluepants, and sandals. At least, the Queen and King wear their gleaming gold crowns with dignity. They hold their heads high, as if their gold crowns were made of scruffbird feathers.

"Morning," mumbles Milli with a full mouth. "These pancakes are really tasty! Rich, but fluffy and light. How does Chef Soofull do it?"

"He's the best," Sharoo agrees, pulling back her chair.

A curly black sheephound crouches beneath the mahogany table, hoping for scraps of bacon. This is Ruffy, Milli's dog Ruffles.

Dark-haired Milli reminds Sharoo of a pert, beady-eyed bird. She was born on the day of the Copper Cat. Bart is chubby, with a face like a boiled golden potato. His birth sign is the Ruby Fox. He has a keen, sometimes kooky sense of humor.

"What's wrong?" says Milli, squinting her sharp little eyes. "You guys look worried."

"Our Floaters gave us a warning," says Clyde. "Invaders from another planet."

Milli gasps. She loves science fiction, but this is real life!

"We'll survive," says Bart. "If we planet right."

Milli giggles nervously.

Sharoo smiles. Bart will joke about anything.

Like a shiny globe, Charlton's ivory head appears. The Chief Steward holds a silver pitcher of coffee and a small one of fresh cream. "Good morning, Your Majesties. What may I serve you for morn-meal?"

"Pancakes, please," says Sharoo.

"Same for me," says Clyde.

"At once." Charlton pours them small cups of coffee, bows, and departs.

Clyde turns to Bart. "This warning is serious," he says. "The invaders are deadly-dangerous."

"Eee!" Milli squeals. "Deadly for us?"

"Apparently so," says Clyde. "Our Floaters were vague."

Milli's eyes widen. "I know! I know what they are!"

"What?" asks Bart.

"They're . . ." She makes a sour face. "I flashed on it, but it slipped away. Something I read about, in an issue of *Mind-Chilling Speculations,* but now I can't remember."

"You'll think of it," Sharoo tells her.

"There's a new memory medicine," says Bart. "It's called Whatzitsname."

Clyde and Sharoo laugh.

"There's nothing we can do about the invaders now," says Clyde, slipping Ruffy a scrap of crispy bacon. "Hey! Why don't we make you a Duke, Bart? The citizens might respect you more when you crack jokes."

"Good idea!" Sharoo exclaims. "And Milli can be a Duchess."

Milli smiles. "But a Duke and Duchess of what? They're always *of something.*"

"Right," says Clyde. "What do you think, Roo?"

"Ruffles," says Bart before she can reply. "The Duke and Duchess of Ruffles. Has a good ring to it."

"Perfect!" Sharoo exclaims. "So be it."

It doesn't occur to anyone that this might make matters worse. The Duke and Duchess of Dog!

Charlton enters smoothly through the swinging door, bringing two large plates of steaming pancakes.

"Meet the Duke and Duchess of Ruffles," Sharoo tells him.

"Indeed?" Charton's eyebrows slightly rise. "It's a great honor." He bows respectfully to the new noble couple. As he glides from the room, he's smiling with amusement.

Bart grins. "If I get into an argument, I can duke it out now."

Clyde groans.

Milli laughs.

"Clyde and I have C.C. today," Sharoo declares. "Maybe you and Milli should preside with us. You're both nobility now." (In Broan, C.C. stands for Citizens' Court.)

"Why not?" says Bart. "It'll be fun to see how you monarchs, in your boundless wisdom, settle citizens' disputes."

Clyde yawns. "It's not for a while yet, and I'm bored." He raises his voice. "Charlton! Summon the Foon!" (On Plash, a foon is a cross between a fox and a raccoon. The animal is highly intelligent, and an excellent mimic.)

Charlton's shiny head appears. "At once, Your Majesty!"

Before long, a snooty servant leads in a furry brown animal—also with a snooty expression. The Foon wears clownish blue clothes with big red buttons, and walks nimbly on his hind legs. He is tethered by a silver chain, which the snooty servant removes.

"The Foon, Your Majesty!" The servant bows.

The Foon bows, too. "Thuh Foon, Yer Majesty!" His voice is growly and rough, but surprisingly clear.

"Foon!" says Clyde. "Have you learned any new tricks?"

"Foon! Have few learn denny new tricks?" The Foon, who understood perfectly, steps forward. He sings in his hoarse, growly voice:

> *Please take egg lance*
> *at my nude ants.*
> *I'll jump and prance!*

The four teenagers laugh. A glance at my new dance!

The Foon laughs happily too. He leaps high in the air, twisting and turning. His jumps are agile, surprisingly graceful.

After a series of whirling gyrations, the animal executes a smooth somersault, landing to make a respectful bow.

King Clyde laughs. "Excellent!"

The Foon laughs too. He is led away muttering, "Egg sell ant!"

)(

"That was quite a performance!" Sharoo exclaims. "He jumped like a kangaroo."

Bart clears his throat. "Anyone know what can jump as high as this castle?"

Blank faces all around.

"A dead foon," says Bart. His face is totally serious.

"You silly!" says Milli. But her voice is affectionate. "A dead foon can't jump!"

Bart smirks. "Neither can this castle."

"Huh?" Milli scrunches up her face.

Sharoo suddenly laughs. "*Both* the castle and a dead foon can't jump. Each one can jump as high as the other."

Milli shakes her head, smiling.

The four teenagers are in a better mood now. The Foon's dance was fun.

They have almost forgotten their fears of an impending invasion.

FOUR

Queen Sharoo and King Clyde sit serenely on their thrones, ready for Citizens' Court. Seen from above, the spikey circles of their round crowns gleam. At one side, the Duchess and Duke are perched on gold-cushioned chairs, smiling expectantly.

Charlton's ivory head leans through the door. "Teacher Amalda Floozi of The Simon Says School, and the Stoobutz family!"

A tall, thin lady enters the room. Her skin is bright green. Her hair, a jumble of blonde curls. She has piercing black eyes, a long, pointed nose, and thin red lips.

The entire Stoobutz family has splotchy pink skin. The wife is short and fat. She looks grumpy and tough. Her stocky husband bows and scowls.

Their son, a sneaky little lad, peeks sourly out from behind his mother's wide skirt.

Queen Sharoo thinks back to when she was a helpless little girl, taught by the sadistic Mr. Sade (who later perished in a giant sinkhole). She studies the tall teacher. "Please state your case."

Miss Floozi points to the boy. "Kirbi here is sassy and impertinent, Your Majesty. He disrupts class and refuses to do any work."

"She hates my guts!" Kirbi whines. "She always calls on me when I'm not prepared."

Kirbi's father slams his son's shoulder.

"Your Highness," the boy sullenly adds.

King Clyde raises his ivory scepter. "Why are you unprepared, Kirbi?"

The boy squirms uneasily. "I do prepare, Your uh Highness. Honest I do. But my head leaks."

Milli stifles a giggle.

Miss Floozi clears her throat. "Kirbi, I'm afraid, is not very bright. I fail to see how he was promoted to my class."

Bart speaks up. "Want to know how to make Kirbi smart? Smack his knuckles with a ruler."

Shocked silence.

Kirbi glares. His parents scowl.

Miss Floozi's lips form a tiny O. "I could never do that," she hastily remarks. "I abhor any form of violence to encourage learning."

"The Duke was joking," says Clyde. "Smart also means sting."

Miss Floozi blushes.

Kirbi breathes with relief.

"There are other problems," Miss Floozi declares. "This naughty boy sat behind Mimi Mither. He couldn't stop playing with her long, orange hair-braid."

Kirbi grins. "It sways like a hay-snake. Liked to hypnotize me."

The teacher frowns. "I moved his desk to the back of the classroom."

"Where I couldn't hear anything!" Kirbi blurts.

"Where the shameless boy now becomes a monster whenever I turn my back. He has a rubber face. The other kids turn around to stare and laugh. It's shameful!"

"He's just saving face," says Bart.

Miss Floozi gives the Duke a pained look.

Queen Sharoo tilts back her head, whispers, listens.

"There seems to be a personality disharmony here," she observes. "This boy should be transferred to Mr. Lofti's class."

Miss Floozi smiles. "Thank you, Your Highness. Your wisdom is higher than the full moon and twice as—"

"Next!" orders King Clyde.

Miss Floozi and the Stoobutz family quickly leave the throne room.

Charlton's shiny head appears. "The other two disputants departed, Your Highness. They decided to settle the case among themselves. It was a doozy, if I may say so." He smiles. "Both parties were brazenly distorting the facts."

"Thank you, Charlton," Sharoo tells him.

The Chief Steward bows and glides from the room.

"Just as well," says Clyde. "We need to meditate. Maybe we'll intuit something about those dangerous invaders."

"Right," Sharoo declares. "Maybe our Floaters will give us a hint."

"Know how to transform Danger?" says Bart. He pauses a beat. "Erase the D." He pauses again. "And if you erase the first letter of Slaughter . . ."

Only Milli laughs.

In their royal suite, the Queen and King diligently meditate.

After a while, they attempt to reach their Floaters.

"Eedoo!" Sharoo whispers. "We need to know more. How can we prepare unless you give us more information?"

Silence.

"Eeroo!" Clyde whispers. "What planet are the invaders coming from? Can't you even tell me that?"

Silence.

Finally, Sharoo stands up. She gives Clyde a kiss on the forehead. "Maybe they'll tell us more when the invaders are close." She sighs. "I'm going to see Mrs. Zaura."

FIVE

The witch-like seer Mrs. Zaura inhabits a cozy guest-room in the east wing of the castle. She was invited to live there by the Queen.

Sharoo quietly knocks.

When the door opens, she glimpses a lone waxlight flickering beside a quarzz crystal. They're standing on a little table against the far wall.

"Sorry. I didn't mean to interrupt."

Mrs. Zaura makes a friendly wave. "Hello, Your Highness. Hello, Eedoo." (The old seer is the only person ever to see Sharoo's Floater.) "Your timing was perfect, dearie. My trance just hit a dead end." She grins. "But I've never heard of a live end, have *you*, hee hee. Come in, please."

Together, they sit at the little round table.

"How come Sniffy didn't greet me?" Sharoo asks.

The old lady's eyes twinkle. "Sniffy went to the sunny meadow in the sky. I only needed him to guard my hut in the forest." She confidentially lowers her voice. "His bark started hurting my throat, don't you know."

Sharoo nods. "Eedoo says invaders might be coming. From another planet."

"Yes. Eebliz told me." The old lady's eyes burn like the waxlight.

"What planet is it?" Sharoo excitedly asks. "Have you seen?"

29

"No, dearie. But I reached a secret U.R.L. and glimpsed two murky humanoid shapes. Eebliz confirmed this."

Sharoo gasps. She knows that U.R.L. stands for Ultra-Rarified Level. "You mean . . ."

"I'm not sure what I mean." Mrs. Zaura rubs her eyes. "Let me take another look. Sometimes I see better with you beside me. After all, you're a rare Silver Dragon." She takes a deep breath, focuses her eyes in the distance beyond Sharoo's head.

They sit in silence for several minutes.

At last, the seer nods. "Aha." She stretches and grins.

"Did you find out which planet?" Sharoo excitedly asks. "I'll bet it's Saturling!" Her eyes are shining. "It has mysterious orange rings."

Mrs. Zaura cackles. "What makes you assume the planet is in our own solar system?"

Sharoo's mouth falls open. "I just thought . . ."

"It seems to be in a P.U.," the old lady announces. (In Broan, that stands for "parallel universe.")

Sharoo stares, wide-eyed. "How do you know?"

"Look." A thin, bony finger points at the base of the waxlight. The drippings form two curving shapes. "That's a P. And a U."

"Hmm." Sharoo squints doubtfully. Maybe a U, but a P?

"Not a very clear P." Mrs. Zaura seems to read her mind. "You have to know how to interpret the wax, dearie. Anyway, I saw it in my trance."

"What can we do?"

"Good question." Mrs. Zaura gazes dreamily into the distance. "I also saw that the Wizard Wombler failed to realize . . . how vulnerable his five magic portals had made Broan. Aliens with advanced technology can detect and use them, by going through a snakehole."

"A what?"

"That's Professor Wizzleford's term. It's like a tunnel between two adjacent universes." The old lady shrugs. "To aliens with the right technology, our little country is like a helpless castle with five wide-open doors. If they intend to invade us, that is."

Sharoo shudders. She feels a little pang of guilt. But why? It's not her fault that in order to save Clyde, her star body had to pass through two of those portals. "Can they be closed?" she wonders aloud.

Mrs. Zaura shrugs. "I'm not sure. I'll go through Wombler's papers again."

"Good luck!" Sharoo leaves to tell Clyde.

That evening, the royal dining hall gloriously blazes with waxlights as usual. Four teenagers sit at one end of the long mahogany table. The Queen and King at one end, side by side. Duchess Milli on Clyde's right, Duke Bart on Sharoo's left.

Seen from above, two of the four hairy globes are ringed with shiny gold crowns.

Ruffy crouches patiently beneath the table, where his nose confirms his hopes. Between the place settings of Milli and Clyde sits a pink saucer piled with fragrant scraps of bacon.

Munching a thick hard-boiled-egg slice spread with glistening caviar, Sharoo tells Milli and Bart what the old seer said.

They listen intently.

When Sharoo mentions a P.U., Bart smirks.

"Sounds smelly."

Clyde groans.

Sharoo tries not to smile. "This is serious, Bart."

He shakes his head. "It can't be Serious. That's the Cat Star in *our* universe."

"Oh, Bart!" Sharoo shakes her head. He's impossible.

SIX

Twoday dawns foggy and misty. The heavy air is still. Atop the castle, soggy banners limply droop.

High in the sky, two frisky dolphin clouds are joined by two more. This time, all four clouds swirl in a near frenzy.

After morn-meal, the four worried teenagers assemble in the throne room for C.C. A distraction will be welcome.

Charlton appears at the door. The Chief Steward's eyes shine merrily, as if he envisions an amusing dispute.

"Dr. Filbert Musti and cosmetic salesman Ali Torch!"

Sharoo and Clyde curiously survey the disputants.

Dr. Musti is fat and bald, with a thin purple moustache. His jaw has at least three olive chins.

Mr. Torch is tall and handsome, with dark eyes set deep in his yellow face. His slick black hair shines like parted silk.

"Who has the complaint?" asks the Queen.

"I do, Your Highness." Mr. Torch takes a step forward and bows.

"Kindly state it."

"Certainly, Highness." He flashes her a handsome smile. "Yesterday I took a shortcut across Dr. Musti's backyard on my way to town. Like I usually do, and—"

"The scoundrel was trespassing," the doctor interrupts. "Your Majesty."

"I am *not* a scoundrel, Your Highness." Mr. Torch's dark eyes flash.

"Please continue," says the King.

"Passing through a grove of elm trees, I was seized by a boa vine."

Clyde and Sharoo lean forward intently. Milli's eyes flash.

A boa vine is half plant, half reptile. Dangling from a tree, the green creature swings slowly forward . . . and lunges, ensnaring its victim in powerful, sticky coils. Then it gradually *absorbs* its prey. The remaining bones are mostly animal ones, but some are found in a bed of rotting clothes.

"Then what?" Sharoo asks, relieved that the man seems intact.

"Dr. Musti wouldn't help me, Your Highness," Mr. Torch replies. "He said I could hang there until I got eaten."

The Queen addresses the doctor. "Is that true? You were willing to let him die just for trespassing on your property?"

"Of course not, Your Majesty. "I only wanted him to sweat a little."

"How did you get loose?" the King asks Torch.

"Musti brought a stepstool and handed me a hatchet, Your Majesty. I used it to chop myself free. But first, the sadist grinned at me for a long time. It was almost too late when I used the hatchet."

"Why did you make him suffer?" asks Sharoo.

"He never returned my grasscutter, Your Highness." The fat doctor wheezes. "And when he did, it was broken."

"Why did you keep it so long?" asks Clyde.

"He never uses it," Torch replies. "His grass is a shaggy night-mare. And his collie dog makes stinky little towers on my lovely lawn, Your Majesty. Please pardon my graphic language."

Clyde turns to the doctor. "Why does your dog do that?"

"Flopsi is a little squeamish, Your Majesty. She doesn't like squatting in my long, prickly grass. But this scoundrel gave her a poisoned bone! I had it tested in the lab."

The King and Queen exchange worried glances. This case keeps getting more complicated.

"That's ridiculous!" Torch exclaims. If the bone was poisoned, why didn't the stupid mutt die?"

Dr. Musti shrugs. "I didn't let her eat it. I snatched it away immediately. But that's not all. I came home early, after a long day of treating my patients, and found this rogue shamelessly smooching my wife!" He glares daggers at the cosmetic salesman.

Mr. Torch flares up. "That's a gross exaggeration!" He smiles a dreamy smile. "But I'll admit that your wife is pleasingly plump."

"It's true, you scoundrel!" The doctor's face is livid with rage. "You two were greedily kissing on my living-room sofa. Like two hungry dogs lapping oxtail soup!"

Sharoo gasps.

"That's a lie," Torch smoothly replies. "Your wife said that she herself bought that sofa at Nearly New. Best investment she ever—"

"Slanderer!" The doctor's eyes bulge with fury.

Torch turns to the King and Queen. "There's an old saying, Your Majesties. 'Jealousy has demented eyes.'"

Sharoo leans forward. "What were you actually doing?"

The salesman smiles. "I was showing Mrs. Musti a sample of the latest lip gloss, Your Highness. It's called Smoocho." He smiles slyly, thinking back. "Will it smear if I kiss someone?" the lady asked. "Fluttered her eyelids too. As you can imagine, I had to show her it was totally smearless."

"Dastardly lecher!" the doctor yells. "You did more than that!"

"He's being smeared," Bart whispers.

Milli giggles.

"Scoundrel!" Musti rushes at Torch, swinging his pudgy fists.

The salesman briskly kicks the doctor's shins.

The doctor howls, taking another fisted swipe.

Blows are landing fast now.

"Guards!" Clyde raises his ivory scepter.

Two burly soldiers rush into the throne room.

"Apprehend these ruffians!" orders the King.

But the skirmish seems to have ended. The two combatants stand panting and glaring.

Clearly, it's time for a verdict.

"Both disputants should bury the hatchet," says Bart. "Beneath the boa vine. Then Dr. Musti must hug his wounded vine. And Mr. Torch should put on some Smoocho and kiss the collie."

Both men gape in disbelief.

"The Duke is jesting," Sharoo tells them. She solemnly raises her hand. "Community service. For the next year, Dr. Musti, you must treat one patient a week free. You, Mr. Torch, must give out a free sample of lip gloss every day. But without proving its smearlessness." She tries not to smile. "For both of you, two hours a week of veracity classes."

The disputants bow and depart.

"Next!" Sharoo calls.

Charlton's bald head appears. The other disputants are gone, Your Highness. They overheard the last case . . . and departed laughing.

SEVEN

Just before mid-meal, a squall of skullflakes comes swirling down! Plash's normal weather features grape-soda rain and diamond-shaped hail, but skullflakes are extremely rare. These flat, frozen flecks lie in your palm just long enough to grin before they melt.

In the castle's kitchen, two servant lads stand beside a window, watching the whirling display.

"Lookit them skullflakes!" says Auff, raking a hand through his shaggy green hair. "They're clickin' against thuh windah."

"Yeah," says Awn. The lad nervously fingers his acne. "They purdict doom for sure."

Auff nods. "My grandpappy told of a time when skullflakes acritly purdicted swarms of biting locusts."

"Yeah?" says Awn. "I heard they augur galloping lepersy."

"Do tell." Auff shivers. "Maybe it's the both."

Over a mid-meal of fried-egg burgers and mango shakes, the four teenagers watch the whirling, frozen skullflakes strike a wide, leaded window. Their faces freeze in alarm.

"Uh-oh," says Clyde.

"You said it," says Bart.

"A squall of skullflakes hit my Aunt Myrtle's house just before she died," Milli declares, sipping a mango shake. "No one had any idea her heart was bad. But the weather on Plash is never wrong."

Below the table, Ruffy whines dolefully, as if he understands.

"Don't we have enough to worry about?" Sharoo wonders aloud.

Bart smirks. "Did you hear about the ambitious skull?" He pauses a beat. "It wanted to get ahead."

Milli laughs.

Bart nods. "What's another name for grave robbing?"

Nobody knows.

"Skullduggery."

Clyde groans.

Sharoo smiles, in spite of herself.

After a long discussion about how to deal with the mysterious invaders, the four teenagers still have no idea what to do.

When asked, Eedoo and Eeroo are silent.

Charlton glides in through the swinging door. "Beg pardon, Your Majesties. Rumors of impending doom are rampant. The people are almost certain to panic."

"Thank you," says Clyde. "We'll handle it." He smiles, but it's not a confident smile.

"Yes, Your Highness." The swinging door swings again.

The skullflakes have stopped now. They slowly melt, grinning in the bright sunlight.

Sharoo muses out loud. "I know. I'll give a speech tomorrow morning to reassure the citizens. I'll give it in Palisades Park."

"Why the park?" asks Milli.

"There will be too many people for Speare Theater to hold."

Sharoo gazes into the distance. "Mayor Skoo says the park is better. People can pass along what I say to the ones out of earshot."

"Nobody shoots ears anymore," quips Bart. "Hey! Why did the doofus sit on a park bench scattering empty candy wrappers?"

Nobody knows.

Bart grins. "There was a sign that said, "FINE FOR LITTERING!"

Milli giggles.

Clyde groans.

Bart's face goes deadpan. "An old man asks the doofus why he's scattering the wrappers. 'To keep the tigers away,' he answers. 'Fool!' the old man says. 'There aren't any tigers around here!' The doofus smiles. 'Effective, isn't it?'"

Clyde snorts.

Sharoo scrapes back her chair. "I need to work on my speech. We've got Astrology with Mrs. Zaura at four."

The Queen climbs the curving stairs, two at a time.

Sitting on a gold cushion in her royal prayer room, she mentally begs Eedoo for inspiration. She also asks the O.B.E. "May I say what is best for the people to hear," she prays. "May they be calm and reassured."

Then she meditates deeply, humbly seeking inner peace.

After that, Sharoo feels better. She now has a sense of what to say. All may yet be well.

But an old Broanian adage pops into her head: "If you think all is well, look behind you."

EIGHT

It's four o'clock.

The Queen, King, Duchess, and Duke gather in the library—a mellow, luxurious room on the ground floor of the castle. Carved mahogany shelves hold rows of gold-embossed volumes. The titles range from Saucer's *Zingberry Tales* to Frank Bomb's *Dotti in the Land of Odd.*

They lounge in magenta armchairs beside a wide oak table with two stained-glass lamps. Bart's sandaled feet splay out lazily on the table's polished surface.

The four teenagers regularly meet here for what they call "Double-A." Professor Wizzleford teaches Astronomy; Mrs. Zaura, Astrology. Today, it's Astrology.

Strangely, Mrs. Zaura hasn't arrived yet.

"Maybe she's planning to moon us," says Bart. "With stars in her eyes."

Sharoo bristles. "Easy, Bart! That's disrespectful."

"Sorry, Roo. I'm a Ruby Fox." He spreads his palms. "What can I say?"

"Well, not *that*." Sharoo's tone forgives him. "You stepped over the line. But I'm sorry I got angry. I'm worried about the invaders."

"And well might you be, hee hee." Mrs. Zaura spryly enters the room. "Apologies for my tardiness. I was trancing intensely." She sinks down into a wheezy leather armchair.

Bart's sandaled feet hit the floor.

"What did you see?" Sharoo anxiously asks.

"Murky figures with strange weapons." The seer sadly shakes her head. "Vortex, the planet of surprise, is in a rare, ominous alignment with Saturling and Blore."

"Blore is blood and gore," says Milli. "But what is Saturling? I forget."

"Ego, dearie. Ego is a false friend, a great obstacle to spiritual progress. And now that the moon is void of course, with mutable fires in the seventh house, the chances are great for a sudden, bloody comeuppance."

Milli's hand flies to her mouth.

"Our citizens are overconfident." Mrs. Zaura sighs. "And we just had a whirligig of skullflakes. As you know, skullflakes portend disaster. Broan, or Plash, apparently deserves one."

Clyde looks puzzled. "How could a planet deserve disaster?"

Mrs. Zaura cackles sadly. "I'm sure you all know the L.O.B." She grins. "The Law of Boomerang says that everything you think or do—sooner or later returns to you."

Everyone nods.

"Well, the L.O.B. functions not only for individuals, but for entire planets."

"Why shouldn't it?" says Bart. "Planets are heavenly bodies."

"What's that? Bodies? Hee hee, I suppose so." Mrs. Zaura grins. "There's a collective Boomerang for everyone on Plash." Her squinting eyes probe the distance. "The Glyzeans, with their cruelty, created negative Boomerang. That was partly why the Morfers came." She raises a bony finger. "The nasty Lollers created still more bad Boomerang. And that contributed to a disaster that only one of you knows about."

Sharoo shudders. The old lady means Clyde's death, of which he himself still has no idea. His terrible, bloody death, which her star body, aided by Mrs. Zaura's magic, went back in spacetime *and prevented*. Sharoo hasn't told him yet, because he was seduced by Blizza, Mrs. Zaura's granddaughter, which he would surely be ashamed to learn, even though the girl had bewitched him with purple magic.

"What disaster was that?' asks Clyde.

Sharoo holds her breath.

"It was prevented," Mrs. Zaura says. "The important thing is that Plash is now in a dangerous configuration. As you know, the planets and stars, according to their alignment, indicate forces at work that modify and intensify our fate." Her eyes gleam. "After we defeated the Glyzeans, Morfers, and Lollers, our people have swelled Egos. They are proud, overconfident, and may soon experience the bad Boomerang from all our drug-addled trippies." (In Broan, trippies are young rebels who smoke rotweed, a drug that gives rise to fantastic visions but slowly rots the brain.)

"As you may know," Mrs. Zaura continues, "my recently reformed granddaughter was a trippie who practiced purple magic." She sighs. "Now she's using her magic skills to help other trippies reform. But they're hooked on rotweed, and smoking rot makes bad Boomerang. Not to mention the thievery, graft, and boozing that are rampant in our land."

Sharoo nods. She's glad that she locked up the mango brandy after Auff and Awn kept sneaking it. Her own parents moved out of the castle because whiskey was too available to her heavily drinking father.

"What can we do?" asks Milli. "We don't take drugs or drink too much."

45

Mrs. Zaura gazes into space, shrugs. "You can't, as they say, lock the cage after the viper escapes. But a law that bans rotweed and limits the sale of alcohol might be helpful."

"Right," Clyde agrees. "I'll draw one up."

"A spirited solution," says Bart.

This time, the old lady makes a sour smile. "Your wit, young man, isn't always constructive. Right now, a great danger is on the way. The best course of action is humble prayer. The O.B.E. isn't deaf, you know." She rises. "That's all for today."

NINE

Threeday is sunny and bright. In the clear blue sky, four dolphin clouds (are they the same ones?) lazily float. They seem to be resting. Are they tired from trying to suggest the future? Have they decided, in their cloudy way, that the skullflakes were warning enough?

In Palisades Park, a huge crowd mills around the hastily built platform. Above a group of laughing young trippies, rising ribbons of rotweed smoke leave a bitter-sweet aroma in the air.

Broan's older citizens argue about the significance of the skullflakes. Many apply their own superstitious spin . . .

"Doom looms!" wails a disheveled man with haunted eyes. "The O.B.E. has been peering into our bedrooms. Doesn't like what happens there."

"Speak for yourself, Kraig," says a hawk-faced man beside him. "In your case, I'll bet the O.B.E. saw plenty."

"That's funny as a flood, Earle," says Kraig. "You'll be burning in The Hot Place soon enough."

"You're both wrong," says an old lady known as Loony Loosi. "Gremlins are crawling out from their underground caverns! Little hairy twitchy ones."

The crowd is restless, like the Shipshape Sea before a storm.

Seven husky soldiers clear a path to the podium. The Queen makes her way through the people, gently slapping "high palms" with enthusiastic fans.

On the platform, a bearded geek inspects a golden microphone, stamped with the black letters Q.S. He turns it over to Mayor Skoo, a lean man with scheming eyes and a graying beard.

Mayor Skoo hides a peculiar smile. He strikes the mike. It makes a loud, metallic sound, and a few people jump. "Quiet, please, citizens of Broan! I know you are concerned about the future of our land. It is my great honor to present your wise and beloved Queen, who will answer your *each and every question.*" The mayor grins slyly. He has never completely forgiven Sharoo for beating him in the royal election, and he knows she doesn't yet have all the answers. "Now, without further ado, Her Majesty Queen Sharoo!"

Thunderous applause fills the air. "Long live the Queen! Hoorah for Queen Sharoo! She'll tell us what to do!"

Sharoo calmly grips the microphone. "Can you hear me?"

The crowd roars. "Yes! Yes!"

"Fine." The Queen tries to look authoritative and reassuring.

"Citizens of Broan! It's true we face a mysterious challenge . . ."

Anxious murmurs ripple through the crowd.

"But we have faced many dangers before." Sharoo's voice rises as she continues. We have overcome the Glyzeans . . . the Morfers from Blore . . . the vicious Lollers . . ."

The citizens cheer each victory. They seem reassured.

Skoo secretly scowls. The clever wench is tooting her own horn!

A fat lady shrilly shouts: "Sharoo always saves us!"

"Yes! I'm totally with her!" cries a tall, thin man.

"She's a phony," a high-pitched, raspy voice complains. "She and the King wear crowns made of lightweight falsa wood, painted gold. They fool most people, but not me."

"Hog slop!" an authoritative voice intones. "Cheap falsa-wood crowns help them remain humble, subdue their Egos. The Queen said so."

"Oh. That's good. I didn't know."

Queen Sharoo confidently smiles. "Yes, we have always been victorious. We have even overcome a disaster you may not be aware of."

The crowd goes silent. People suspiciously whisper.

"What was it?"

"Shush! She'll tell us."

Sharoo twitches. Maybe she shouldn't have said that. She hurriedly continues.

"Good citizens! We now face another formidable challenge. But there is no need for worry. This too will be surmounted! All will be well."

People begin to grumble. "What is the new danger?" they ask.

"Yes, tell us!" they harshly cry.

A wave of resentment grows.

Sharoo feels trapped. The adoration turned to anger so quickly! Should she tell them you can't know an unknown? This wasn't supposed to happen!

For some reason, her glance falls on a tousle-haired, dark-skinned man. A tiny boy, legs dangling, is perched upon his shoulders. The boy seems angry, and the man looks familiar, but she can't place him.

He is Trillbar, the brigand who shot the former King and Queen and was mostly shown mercy by Sharoo—but she fails to realize this. Her mind is trying to recall the words she carefully planned to say. Words now melting away like sand castles on a foamy shore.

"Eedoo!" she whispers. "What should I tell them?"

No answer.

An impatient chant ripples through the crowd: "Tell us! Tell us!"

Tell them to pray. Fervent prayer will help.

The Queen raises her hand. A hush descends.

"My dear citizens, you must pray. Pray to the O.B.E., and all will be well. "My Floater Eedoo tells me that the impending danger can be avoided by fervent prayer."

The citizens murmur uncertainly. They know that Eedoo has helped Sharoo to save them in the past. Many are praying already.

The Queen takes a deep breath. She gets an idea, quickly continues. "Prayer, plus the tactical measures that our undercover agents are taking, will be triumphant!"

The response is better, but still mixed. What undercover agents? Where are they?

Loud voices argue back and forth.

"She still didn't tell us what the danger is!"

"Who cares, if she puts an end to it?"

"The Queen's bluffing. She doesn't have any idea what the danger is!"

"She can't tell us, bump-head. It's a military secret!"

"Where's the King, anyway?"

"Meeting with the undercover agents, lame-brain!"

"Pray, my friends!" Sharoo raises her hands, receiving a moderate cheer. "Ready your weapons! And remain alert!" She descends from the platform.

Mayor Skoo smiles a self-satisfied smile. The upstart wench was squirming plenty!

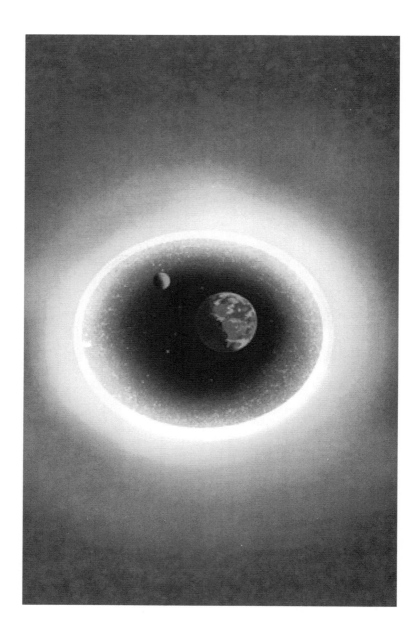

TEN

Fourday is windy. Across the azure sky, puffy white clouds look like clusters of popcorn. The sun splashes them with golden butter.

High above the castle, two frisky gray dolphin clouds make sudden swoops. They seem to be chasing each other—or playing Hide and Find.

Poised on purple cushions in the royal bedchamber, Sharoo and Clyde diligently meditate. Seen from above, they resemble a pair of cross-legged sorcerers, floating on thick magic carpets.

After a while, they stop and stretch. They whisper urgent questions to their Floaters.

Eedoo and Eeroo say nothing.

Morn-meal is a somber affair. Charlton glides in and out of the dining hall like a silent ghost.

The four royal teenagers are lost in thought. They idly pick at tasty scromelets (scruffbird-egg omelets). They nibble warm sweetcrusts and sip strong coffee.

No one says anything.

Below the table, Ruffy softly whines.

Milli slips him a long bacon strip. He gobbles it down.

Sharoo drains the last of her mango juice and wipes her mouth.

"I'm going to see Mrs. Zaura," she announces. "Maybe her trancing has discovered something."

Sharoo hurries along the wide hall of the castle. Gold-framed portraits of previous kings and queens blur past. Do their haunting spirits hover? Are they worried about Broan's future? The Queen has no time to wonder. She climbs the curving marble steps two at a time.

After four knocks, Mrs. Zaura's door swings open.

"Hope I'm not too early," says Sharoo.

The old seer cackles. "Broken broomsticks, no! I've been trancing for a long while." She peers above the Queen's head. "Morning, Eedoo."

Sharoo smiles. "Eedoo returns your greeting. "What did you see in your trance?"

"Plenty. I was just going to send for you. Come in, dearie."

As usual, they sit at the little round table. The glowing quarzz crystal reflects a single, flickering waxlight.

Mrs. Zaura's eyes gleam. She raises a bony finger. "First, I discovered how Wizard Wombler died. It was the strain of setting up the portals. And the exhaustion of casting a protective spell around Plash."

Sharoo gapes. "I thought I made up that spell!"

Mrs. Zaura smiles very strangely. "There actually was one," she says. "But it wore off long before you invented the idea."

"Oh. Then I needed to fool the Morfers anyway." Sharoo rolls her eyes. "Did you find out anything about the invaders?"

The seer stares at the Queen, a little sadly. "I'm coming to that.

I saw that they will probably come from a planet called Earth."

Sharoo's eyes widen. "I remember! You had a glimpse of that planet years ago. Earth is in a P.U."

"Yes, dearie. And now it seems that earthlings called Loopers, in a little country called Loopistan, have developed the technology for inter-dimensional travel."

Sharoo gapes. "They can travel from one universe to another?"

"Yes. Their portals can connect with ours. Their leader is man called Ivan Kisakowski."

Sharoo giggles. "Seriously? Kiss a cow?"

"What else would you expect from a planet called Earth?" Mrs. Zaura cackles, then turns serious. "Kisakowski is ruthless and greedy. These Loopers are scientifically advanced, but morally, not so much. Their Secret Service plans to send soldier-scouts through one of Wombler's portals. They will probably arrive at the castle soon."

Sharoo gasps. "Have you found a way to close the portals yet?"

"No. That may be hard to do. Wombler intended them to be permanent." She looks piercingly at the Queen. "Wombler's magic was very powerful."

"What do these Loopers want?"

The old lady squints. "I'm not sure. But their mission is not a peaceful one. I feel certain about that."

Sharoo smiles grimly. "That was predicted by our Floaters . . . and by the skullflakes." She thinks for a moment. "What do they look like?"

"Sort of like Broanians, I think. I'll keep trancing." She gazes at the Queen again. "Have you told Clyde your secret yet?"

Sharoo shakes her head. "No. I'm still waiting. Things are good between us now. I don't want to upset the mango cart."

The seer nods. "I don't blame you, dearie."

That evening, as usual, the castle's great dining hall blazes with waxlights. It ought to seem festive, but everyone is thoughtful and anxious.

Chef Soofull has prepared a splendid eve-meal of roast pheasant, caramel sweet potatoes, and zingberry salad, but the King and Queen barely notice. The Duke and Duchess of Ruffles also eat mechanically.

After Charlton serves the mango frost-cake, Sharoo takes a deep breath and announces: "Mrs. Zaura said there will be an invasion. Soldier-scouts from a planet called Earth in a P.U. She had a glimpse of that planet before. Anyone remember?"

"I do!" cries Milli. "We all laughed at the name."

"Right," says Bart. "Earth sounds like a dirty, muddy planet."

Sharoo sighs. "Well, earthlings called Loopers, in a country called Loopistan, have discovered the portals. They look sort of like us."

Bart smirks. "Are they loopy?" he says. "Are they out of the loop?"

Clyde smiles grimly. "Who knows? But we'd better find a way to stop them."

ELEVEN

It's dawn on a gloomy gray Fiveday. In the pinkish sky above the castle, two dolphin clouds aggressively frolic.

Soon they are joined by two more.

The royal bedchamber gradually fills with pale, cold light. A duet of deep, steady breathing can be heard.

Lying side by side, the King and Queen awaken to a soft, clunking sound. They stretch, yawn . . . and gasp. Their sleepy eyes go wide.

Two spooky figures in silver-blue space suits stand at the foot of the bed, silently watching. The windows of their helmets are shadowy. Their faces can't be seen. The taller invader points a weird-looking pistol at the bed.

Sharoo grabs Clyde's arm. She's too frightened to talk. These must be the soldier-scouts! Her imagination races, inspired by Milli's retelling of science fiction tales. Are they horrible monsters? Is that a deadly ray-gun? Mrs. Zaura thought the Loopers look like us, but maybe they don't . . .

Clyde is also staring at the soldier-scouts. Should he go for the pistol in his bedside table? No. He might get shot before he could even pull the drawer open.

A gruff, muffled grunt issues from the shorter space suit. The figure reaches up and unscrews his helmet. He slings it onto a chair.

The taller intruder does the same. Apparently, they have decided that the air is breathable.

Sharoo stares. The two intruders look a lot like ordinary men of Broan. Mrs. Zaura was right!

Clyde appraises them. Brutish thugs, slightly wolflike. Bushy eyebrows overhang gleaming eyes. They're staring intensely at Sharoo.

The Loopers grin. Their long, bristly jaws seem to be snarling. They converse in a weird, alien tongue. It sounds like harsh gibberish. Like they're trying to sing with their mouths full of rotweed.

Sharoo catches a few phrases like "Doh-doo-lug." She shudders. The men's eyes are creepy. They're staring at her silky, royal-purple pajamas. "Clyde! Do something!"

"I can't, Roo. That gun looks powerful."

The invaders seem surprised. They turn to each other.

"Par-lee-yut ang-lee-ski!"

"Yah!"

A prickly silence fills the royal bedchamber.

The tall alien waves his weapon. "You speak Inglitch."

Inglitch? The King and Queen say nothing. That seems best.

"Vee . . . Loopers," the short man says. "Vee speak Inglitch too. But only leetle."

"Why are you here?" says Clyde. "What do you want?"

The tall man hisses: "Vee seek meeny rahls." He turns to the other man. "Krant, yak zo ang-lee-ski *gola-dor*?"

"Golt," the short man replies. Vee vahnt golt. Alzo udder meeny rahls."

Clyde understands. North of Broan city, beneath the Snowpeak Mountains, lie rich veins of mineral deposits.

"Vee vill need . . ." Krant pauses. ". . . slayfs to verk."

Clyde shivers.

"How did you get here?" asks Sharoo.

"True zee portal," says Krant. "Vee land in hall near old woman door."

"Mrs. Zaura!" Sharoo exclaims.

"She vake up," says the tall man. "She now dead on rug."

"Yii!" Sharoo squeals. "No!"

"You not skreem!" the tall man growls. "Udder people come, vee keel dem." He turns to Krant. "Yak zo ang-lee-ski floyk?"

"Faint. Old woman faint on rug."

Sharoo feels a wave of relief. Mrs. Zaura might still be alive!

The short man glances at the shiny gold crowns hanging on the bedposts. He too is fooled by them. "You are Kink ant Kveen?"

Clyde gulps. "Yes, but . . ."

The tall man grins at Sharoo. "Out of zee bed."

Sharoo doesn't move.

"Out!" His rough voice trembles with anger. "I show vhat vee can do. I keel table." He aims his bulging pistol at the gold-trimmed desk standing against the wall.

Krahist! A crackling stream of yellow-white light strikes the desk.

Instantly, it becomes a bright square of fire.

Seconds later, only a lumpy, smoking pile remains.

Sharoo and Clyde helplessly gape.

The ray-gun points at the Queen's face. "Out!"

Sharoo climbs out of bed. She stands beside it, trembling.

The two men stare at her purple monogrammed pajamas.

The tall one winks at the short one. "Ploofnah, Krant."

The short one grins. "Yah, Vozhi." His laugh is guttural and ugly. "Kveen, it zeems, has zee pleasing body."

Clyde almost rushes them, but wisely holds back.

The room is becoming lighter. Sharoo thinks desperately. She can read the men's eyes. It's clear what they intend to do.

She makes a quick, fervent prayer to the O.B.E. And to Eedoo. *Please, please help!*

The tall man waves his ray-gun in impatient little circles. "You vill now remove sleep-suit."

Sharoo hesitates. A wild idea pops into her head.

"Why not?" she blurts. "You are very handsome men. I was getting tired of the King anyway."

Clyde can't believe his ears. "Roo! No!"

The men leer expectantly at Sharoo.

She smiles seductively at Vozhi, then at Krant.

"No!" cries Clyde, but somehow manages to stay back. If they shoot him, he can't help Sharoo.

"I keel zis doh-doo-lug," says Vozhi, pointing his ray-gun at Clyde.

"Nah," Krant objects. "Vee need kink to get slayfs."

Clyde rises up on the bed. "Why, you . . ." But Vozhi's ugly pistol holds him back.

"Oh, I feel sooo hot!" Sharoo sexily murmurs. She starts unbuttoning her pajama top.

The invaders watch with saucer-like eyes.

Clyde looks on in helpless horror.

Sharoo abruptly stops disrobing. "You two take off those stupid suits." She flutters her eyes. "Who wants to be first?"

"I first!" Vozhi savagely cries.

"No, I first!" Krant's eyes gleam.

They glare at each other, eagerly fumbling with their spacesuits. Vozhi, still holding his weapon, is slower.

Quick as a viper-snake, Sharoo snatches Krant's ray-gun from its holster.

Krahist! Krahist! Two crackling streams of yellow-white light strike out, one after the other.

Vozhi explodes in a flash of fire. Then Krant.

"Yay!" Clyde, smiling, waves his fist triumphantly.

Sharoo almost faints. She numbly lowers the ray-gun.

Two piles of smoking matter decorate the floor.

"Roo!" Clyde embraces her. "That was so risky! The odds were a zillion to one that they'd—"

"But it worked, thank the O.B.E." Sharoo's voice is weak and shaky. "I had to get them arguing. What other choice did I have? They both wanted me. And they would have killed *you*."

Clyde smiles with relief. "You were really convincing. *I was getting tired of the King.* He laughs nervously. I almost believed you."

Sharoo's face turns sad, but only for a second. "Mrs. Zaura!" she cries. "Let's check on her! Quick!"

They rush out through the bedchamber door.

TWELVE

The Queen and King race to the east wing of the castle. The door of Mrs. Zaura's room stands half open.

They find the old lady lying on the rug—just as the Loopers said.

The seer's eyes are closed. Her expression is calm, but her mouth looks shockingly lopsided. A wooly black nightgown is bunched up above her knobby knees.

Sharoo drops to the floor. The old woman's chest is moving gently. She's still breathing!

"Mrs. Zaura!" Sharoo exclaims.

No answer.

Clyde saturates a facecloth in the water room. He carefully applies it to the old lady's forehead. Her wrinkled eyelids flutter open. "Curdled cauldrons! What happened?"

"You fainted," Sharoo tells her. "We think." She studies the seer's face. "But I blasted the Loopers with their own ray-gun."

Mrs. Zaura sits up. She's wide awake now. "Oh yes. The Loopers."

Sharoo shudders. "Invaders in silver spacesuits. They came for gold. But first, they were going to . . ."

"You don't need to say." The old seer sadly blinks her eyes. "I just had a vision of them." She grins. "You turned them into smoky puddles. That was quick thinking, dearie."

Mrs. Zaura slowly rises to her feet. She pulls on the tapestry strip beside her bed. "I need some hot water for my revitalizing tea," she says. "And a light morn-meal. After that, I will search through the Wizard Wombler's old papers. Those portals must be closed!"

"You sure you're all right?" Sharoo regards her anxiously.

"Good as gold. So to speak." The old seer smiles. "Takes more than a scare to break my old bones."

Sharoo and Clyde return to the royal bedchamber.

Two charred piles lie on the rug, side by side.

The King and Queen ring for Charlton.

Wide-eyed, he leaves to fetch a clean-up crew.

The King and Queen meditate in Clyde's former bedroom.

Eedoo's voice sounds softly in Sharoo's head. *Good work.*

"Why did they keep saying Doh-doo-lug?" she whispers.

That means fool. They called Clyde that.

"What about Ploofnah?"

That was you. It is said . . . of fresh warm bread.

"I'm glad I blasted them."

They were living beings, but you had no choice.

Sharoo frowns. "They were bad living beings."

Earthlings have the potential for much good, but their moral progress has lagged behind their scientific advancements.

At this moment, Eeroo is telling Clyde: *You had a narrow escape. And you are about to learn a secret.*

"How?" Clyde whispers. "When?"

Silence.

The Queen and King feel a rush of relief. They were cold and numb with fear, but now, they're awash with warm gratitude.

Sharoo kisses Clyde, saying she has something to tell him.

Clyde smiles. "I know."

"You know my secret!?"

"No. But Eeroo just said I would learn one."

Sharoo rolls her eyes. "Well, your Floater was right. Remember Blizza? How she acted so well in the play?"

"Yeah."

Sharoo takes a deep breath. "In another reality, she seduced you."

"What!? No way." Clyde's head is spinning. "Another reality?"

"Yes. The way things *were*. But you couldn't help it. She used purple magic to enchant you."

"What!?"

"And when I stopped her, she stabbed you with a dagger. And you died."

Clyde stares in alarm. "Roo, have you been smoking rot?"

"No, but here's what happened . . .

She tells an astonished Clyde how her star body, aided by Mrs. Zaura, traveled back in spacetime, passed through two of Wombler's magic portals, and managed to prevent his death.

Clyde is stunned. He quickly tilts back his head. "Eeroo!" he whispers. "Is that true?"

The answer stuns him even more. *Yes. You should believe Sharoo. She will always be truthful with you.*

Clyde gasps. He gives Sharoo a big, loving hug.

"You can ask Mrs. Zaura if you want," she says, smiling.

"No. I trust Eeroo. And you," he quickly adds.

Sharoo fills him in with more details. "But you must never tell anyone," she solemnly declares. "That is our secret now. Only Mrs. Zaura knows."

THIRTEEN

At morn-meal, the Queen and King tell the Duchess and Duke what happened with the Loopers.

Milli's beady eyes stretch wide.

"How did we sleep through all that?" Bart wonders aloud.

"I heard something scary in my sleep," says Milli. "I thought it was a nightmare."

Clyde's expression is serious. "Those portals need to be closed! Before any other aliens come through!"

Sharoo recalls the seer's words: *like a helpless castle with five wide-open doors.* "You're right," she says, standing up. I'll go see Mrs. Zaura. She's searching for a way to close them."

Hurrying along the hallway, Sharoo vaguely notices the portraits of previous queens and kings. As usual, their dignified faces stare serenely out from wide gold frames. But today the wall seems unusually shiny. For an instant, something seems to shimmer.

Could a ghost be haunting these rows of ancient rulers? If so, it's probably Queen Reeya. She was always kind and loving to Sharoo.

With Reeya's gentle face in mind, the girl takes the curving marble steps two at a time.

)(

After only two knocks, Mrs. Zaura's door swings open. The old lady seems excited.

"Good news, Your Majesty! The Wizard Wombler left instructions for a spell to close the portals. The parchment was hidden. He hoped the closing spell would never be used."

Sharoo smiles. "But now we need it. How soon can you work it?"

"Almost immediately." The old seer grins. "But your star body will face some risks again. Sit down, please."

Sharoo is dumbstruck. "My . . . star body?"

"Yes, dearie. Please sit down."

They sit at the little table with the crystal, and Mrs. Zaura lights the lone waxlight.

"Your very own star body. Hee hee." The old woman cackles hoarsely. "Once again, it needs to be someone in touch with a Floater. There's a good chance that the King could—"

"No! Not Clyde." Sharoo shudders. "I already lost him once! I was hoping you could work the closing spell by yourself."

"How would I send *my own* star body? But if you do it, I'll be helping you." She eyes Sharoo intensely.

"What will I have to do?"

The old woman grins. "It's roughly the same procedure as before. With some of the same risks. But no magic circle. We won't be altering any history, hee hee. This time, your star body will *stay inside* the portals, without passing through them." She gently pats Sharoo's arm. "You've traveled this way before, so it should be easier now."

Sharoo thinks of Clyde, of the people of Broan. And of the unknown risks. "Isn't there any other way?" Her head is reeling.

"I'm afraid not, dearie. I've been trancing like a cobra snake. I saw that other aliens might soon invade us. Some were . . . unscrupulous and predatory." Her voice is grim. "There is no doubt about it. The portals must be closed as quickly as possible."

Sharoo gasps, slowly nods.

"All right. Let's do it."

FOURTEEN

Mrs. Zaura pulls a crumbly yellowed parchment from the trunk at the foot of her bed. "The old slyboots magically stuck it between two boring little spells, so it wouldn't be easy to find, don't you know." She grins. "A charm for diminishing gossip and one for removing warts." She cackles softly.

"But I found it." She waves the parchment, sits down beside the Queen. "I'll study it once more, to be absolutely certain."

Sitting at the little table, Sharoo patiently waits.

Soon the old seer sighs. "Ah, yes. I think I can make it work."

Soon she is mixing magic ingredients with purified water in a glass vial. Sharoo thinks she sees some different powders this time. As before, Mrs. Zaura shakes the vial, places it upright on a wooden stand.

"Now." She unfurls the parchment. "Here is Wombler's spell for closing the portals: *Plash opening! Return to a lasting slumber!* Your star body must *think this spell* beside each of the five portals."

Sharoo memorizes the spell. She recites it three times perfectly.

The old seer nods. "Good. If anything goes wrong, think the word *Odnu.*"

"Odnu?" Sharoo wrinkles her brow. "What does that mean?"

"It's '*undo*' backwards, hee hee."

Sharoo laughs. "That's clever. I wish I'd thought of it."

"You did, dearie. You did." Mrs. Zaura thinks this, but doesn't say it. Instead, she says aloud: "Wombler was a very clever Wizard. In the spell itself, the first letters of the words spell *portals*."

Sharoo's eyes grow wide. "He *was* clever!"

Mrs. Zaura studies her carefully. Is that the ghost of a remembrance? "If you undo the spell, you must redo it, of course."

"Of course." Sharoo's head is still reeling.

"The potion is ready now." The old woman holds out the vial."

Sharoo takes a deep breath, drinks it all in one gulp. This time, the thick liquid tastes a little sweeter. "Not bad."

"You're getting a taste for it, hee hee. Now we must sit in meditation. As before, you will slip into a dream, but you will be *aware* that you are dreaming. Your star body will then be released."

They both sit quietly on gold cushions, their eyes closed.

Sharoo feels a familiar tingling vibration. She hears a whistling sound, feels "herself" being pulled away from her body.

Mrs. Zaura was right. It's much easier this time. Easy as greasy! (A common Broanian expression.)

The hovering StarSharoo (as she now thinks of herself) can see perfectly, even though her flesh body's eyes are closed. She can see herself and Mrs. Zaura, sitting on cushions on the floor. She is *differently* conscious.

StarSharoo floats freely. She rushes through churning nonspace. Through chaotic ether. As before, the air seems strangely alive.

Now, what was she supposed to do? Something important, but what? She struggles to recall.

Like last time, StarSharoo has a glimmer of Eedoo's paradox: You must have self-reliance but depend on a higher power. Self-reliance without Ego. She humbly, earnestly prays to the O.B.E.

There. It's coming back now. Close the five portals.

Already she sees three of them in the distance . . .

StarSharoo begins with the portal farthest away. Gliding up close, she thinks the closing spell. *Plash opening! Return to a lasting slumber!*

At the word "slumber," the portal hisses like a punctured balloon, closing in upon itself. Within a few seconds, it disappears entirely.

StarSharoo smiles. Piece of tortlet!

Four portals remain. StarSharoo floats to the next portal. She has more control of her star body this time. She hurries, thinking of Mrs. Zaura's words. "The portals must be closed as quickly as possible."

StarSharoo expertly closes the next three, saving the one near the castle for last. That's where she wants to end up.

Almost finished. She increases the pace still more.

Ow! As the last portal hisses shut, her left star-leg gets caught. It's firmly clamped! Unable to move. In her haste, a leg slipped into the closing portal.

The opening has shrunk, but hasn't disappeared. It's like a pale mouth, biting her!

StarSharoo wrenches and struggles in vain. She was overconfident. Too much Ego! There's an old Broanian saying: Overconfidence courts calamity.

StarSharoo can't even budge her star-leg!

Wait! There's a magic word to cancel the spell. What is it? No-nu? No. Do-nu? No. Her panicky star-mind can't remember! Her star-memory isn't like her flesh memory. She can't access it!

Her star-leg hurts worse and worse. It's really bad now! Star

Sharoo grimaces with pain. She prays frantically, humbly to the O.B.E. What *is* that word to undo the— Oh, yes. Odnu!

She thinks the word fiercely, and it frees her, just as the pain was becoming unbearable.

Making sure that she is free of the portal, StarSharoo rethinks the closing spell . . . and easily maneuvers herself back to the castle, beside Mrs. Zaura.

Whew!

The old seer has a pained expression. Evidently, she was "tuned in" to Sharoo's star body.

"That was careless, dearie."

Sharoo frowns. "I'm sorry. It was easy, and I got overconfident. Lost my concentration. My left leg really hurts."

"That will soon go away." Mrs. Zaura smiles sympathetically. "The important thing is that all the portals are closed. You did it, dearie!"

"I did, didn't I?" Sharoo smiles with relief. "Hooray!"

Her leg feels normal. She rushes to tell Clyde.

Striding past the gold-framed portraits in the hall, Sharoo senses a subtle movement at the periphery of her vision. Something shiny and cold. But when she tries to focus on it, there's nothing there. If it's a ghost, it's a persistent one!

Clyde is happy with the news, but Sharoo doesn't describe exactly what *she* did. She gives total credit to Mrs. Zaura's magic. If she told Clyde about StarSharoo, he might get angry that she took so much risk again.

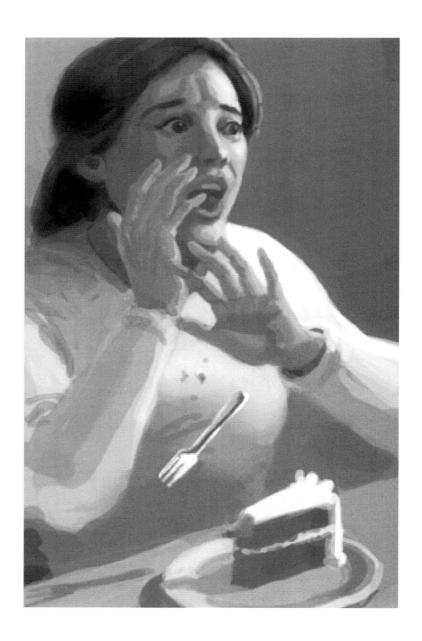

FIFTEEN

At mid-meal, Sharoo tells Milli and Bart that Mrs. Zaura magically closed all the portals.

Milli cheers.

Bart claps. "Did she use clothes pins?" he asks.

Sharoo smiles. The joke is a welcome distraction from her own part in the procedure.

As if Chef Soofull sensed the need for a celebration, he has created a special surprise dish. Leafy scruffbird-egg salad, sprinkled with reddish-brown cinnamon, zingberries, snoods, and a mysterious tangy dressing. Washed down, of course, with thick mango shakes.

Milli likes it. Bart, not so much. "Salad is for rabbits and women," he says, pushing his plate away. "I'm gonna stuff on mango ice cream and frost-cake."

Clyde is staring at the wall. Something seemed to shimmer there! But when he focused closely, it was gone. It's amazing what you sometimes think you see from the corner of your eye.

Sharoo suddenly gapes. Above the polished mahogany sideboard, something dimly flashes. "What in the name of the O.B.E. is that?"

"Is what?" asks Milli.

"Nothing, I guess. Nothing I can see now." Sharoo's eyes are wide. Was it that shiny ghost again? She has a creepy, suspicious feeling that they're being watched.

"Seems like that *nothing* was really something!" Bart pushes a chunk of frost-cake into his already crowded mouth. Since moving into the castle, he's been putting on weight.

"It's gone now," Sharoo declares, squinting.

The unrecognizable Loopers are scraped up and buried behind the castle. The four teenagers say a brief, half-hearted prayer for their spirits.

In the royal bedchamber, the Queen and King gratefully meditate. They thank the O.B.E. They thank their Floaters, too. Sharoo's gratitude is more complete, but Clyde's is no less earnest.

After a long time, Sharoo stretches.

Excellent meditation. Eedoo's voice is warm and friendly.

The Queen smiles. "With the portals closed, it was easier to concentrate."

Unfortunately, two other aliens came through.

Sharoo gasps. "That's impossible!"

"What's impossible?" says Clyde.

"The portals are . . . all closed." Sharoo's voice is shaky. "But Eedoo says two other aliens came through."

Clyde quickly tilts back his head, whispers, listens. "Eeroo says they came through before the portals were closed."

"More Loopers?" he whispers toward the ceiling. Then he gapes. "Eeroo says no. They are creatures from yet another planet."

Now Sharoo tilts back her head. "What are they like?"

Both Floaters answer simultaneously. *Worse than the Loopers. Vicious creatures with evil intentions.*

"Yii!" Sharoo grimaces. "What should we do?"

No reply.

Clyde closes his eyes. "Where are they?" he whispers.

Again, both Floaters answer. *They came through the same portal beside the castle.*

Clyde's eyes grow wide. "Are they in the castle now?"

Silence.

"Help us!" Sharoo cries. "Please!"

Be alert. Mrs. Zaura might help.

"Thanks!" She turns to Clyde. "I'm going to see Mrs. Zaura. You wait here."

"Don't do anything dangerous!" Clyde calls after her, as if he somehow suspects what her star body recently did.

Sharoo races down the corridor. Panic adds wings to her feet.

Mrs. Zaura's door opens at the first pound.

"More aliens! Evil! Vicious!"

"I know," the old seer says. "Eebliz told me. I've been trancing. I could see two dim shapes, a little larger than Ruffy. I sensed that they have big mouths full of sharp teeth. Powerful crusty legs and curvy, tentacle-like arms. Their appendages can stick to walls, like those of spiders or flies."

Sharoo shudders. "What can we do to capture them?"

Mrs. Zaura sighs. "Eebliz won't say. I'll keep trancing."

Sharoo runs back and tells Clyde.

They pray to the O.B.E. They meditate intensely. "Where are the other invaders?" they ask their Floaters. "What should we do?"

No answer.

The silence is eerie.

Worse than the Loopers. The words echo in their heads. *Vicious creatures with evil intentions.*

Sharoo meditates still more intensely. She's not relaxed enough, but how can she be?

Clyde keeps whispering: "What should we do?"

Finally, Eeroo answers: *Stay vigilant.*

"Thanks." Clyde smiles wryly. As if he wasn't!

At eve-meal, they whisper the terrible news to Milli and Bart.

They gasp, wide-eyed.

For once, Bart is tongue-tied.

Serving the roast pheasant, Charlton senses that something is wrong. "Is there anything I may do for Your Majesties?"

"No, thank you," Clyde tells him.

Sharoo squirms nervously. "Just stay alert. Our Floaters say a terrible danger might be coming." She raises a finger. "But don't tell anyone. The people might panic."

"My lips are sealed, Your Highness." A dish rattles slightly on the Chief Steward's tray.

Nibbling a piece of mango frost-cake, Milli suddenly squeals. Crumbs shower down. "What was that?" she cries.

"What was what?" says Bart.

"Ug . . . Ug . . . Against the wall," she stammers. "Something shimmered, but now it's gone!" She shivers. "It seemed c-cold."

"Fright has wild eyes," Bart remarks. He laughs hollowly. "Maybe it's the spirits of those *blasted* Loopers."

Milli giggles nervously. She has a creepy feeling that if she looks away, the shimmery thing will *return.*

"I saw something too," says Clyde. "Over by the door. The wall seemed to ripple slightly. But only for a second."

"A play of light," Bart suggests. "Light can be very playful."

"That's not it," Sharoo tells him. "I saw something shiny before, in the hall. I think it's real." She gulps. "Or else we're so frightened, we're *seeing things.*"

Now Bart detects a shimmer. He squints at the wall. "I *see* what you mean!"

The mysterious *shimmerings* subside.

But the teenagers are no less worried. They go to their bed-chambers directly after eve-meal . . . and lock the heavy oak doors.

Sharoo prays to the O.B.E. for a long time.

Clyde goes to bed with the surviving Looper ray-gun on his bedside table.

But he can't fall asleep. He's staying vigilant.

SIXTEEN

It's early Sixday morning, just after midnight. In the dark-indigo sky, a crescent of yellow hangs like a curving dagger-blade.

Viewed from above, the castle seems to crouch like a gigantic shadowy beast. Inside, it is almost totally dark.

A sharp crash rends the air. The door of Milli's bedchamber splinters apart! Ruffy leaps from the bed, barking furiously.

A stealthy shape, as dark as the darkness itself, leaps down from the wall. It silences the sheephound, drags him out into the hall. Ruffy lies still.

Clyde, who hasn't slept at all, is already there. He holds the ray-gun in his right hand, a battery-powered torch in his left. Its beam illuminates the senseless dog, his stiff legs stretched sideways.

"What's happening?" Sharoo has followed him. "Yii!"

Clyde stares in horror. With a shaky hand, he aims the torch above Ruffy, where an ugly creature looms. The monster blinks on and off, like a faulty neon sign. Its eyes viciously gleam.

Milli appears, wearing a light-blue nightdress. "Nooo!" she screams. Heedless of the monster, she plunges forward to save Ruffy.

"Fark!" Without thinking, Clyde utters a crude curse word. He quickly aims the ray-gun at the ugly creature blinking above Milli and Ruffy.

Krahist! A stream of yellow-white light shoots out.

The monster flares up in a fiery blob. It falls to the floor in a sizzling, smoking heap.

Milli hugs Ruffy's lifeless body. He's bleeding! He—" She slumps down beside him, and says no more.

"Milli!" Sharoo gasps. "What's wrong?"

Bart arrives in bright-red pajamas. He gasps. "What thuh—"

"I blasted it!" cries Clyde. "Whatever it was." His torch-beam swings from Milli and Ruffy to the lumpy, smoking heap.

The guard from the front door appears. "Your Majesties! What can I do?" He holds a pistol in his hand.

"Nothing," Sharoo tells him. "The King killed the . . . creature."

Clyde shines his torch on Milli and Ruffy.

"Milli!" cries Bart. "Wake up!"

Everyone seems frozen now.

All of a sudden, the black sheephound twitches. And whimpers.

"He's alive!" Sharoo cries, dropping to her knees. "Milli! Ruffy's alive!"

But her friend lies still as a statue. "Milli!" she cries. "Wake up! Say something!"

No answer.

Ruffy whines again.

Sharoo tilts back her head. "Eedoo! What should I do?"

Wait. The venom on the dog touched her. She will soon wake up, just as Ruffy did.

"What? You mean, Milli's all right?"

Yes. The creature's venom renders its prey unconscious. You must let it evaporate. Don't touch the dog for a few minutes. His wounds are superficial.

Sharoo tells the others.

They nod with relief, and wait.

Sprawled on the floor, Milli soon wakes up.

She's overjoyed to find Ruffy alive. Before anyone can stop her, she happily grabs him . . . and falls back again, unconscious.

"Fark!" Clyde mutters under his breath. "Nobody touch her. And don't let Ruffy touch you!"

They all wait.

This time, Milli regains consciousness faster.

Sharoo makes her sit still for a few minutes.

Ruffy whimpers beside them while they talk.

Milli suddenly squeals. "Didn't Eedoo say that *two* other aliens came through?"

"Yes!" Sharoo quickly tilts back her head and whispers. "Eedoo! Where's the other one?"

Silence.

Clyde tries too.

No response.

Clyde sends the guard back to the front door with orders to shoot any creature, or shimmer, on sight.

Covered with blankets, the four teenagers, plus Ruffy, spend the rest of the night in the royal bedchamber. The humans take turns passing the ray-gun back and forth so that one of them can stand watch.

Milli gets a wet washcloth, cleans Ruffy's scrapes. They are indeed superficial.

The lights stay on, but the walls reveal no shimmers.

Nobody sleeps a wink.

SEVENTEEN

At last, a welcome Sixday sun breaks through the wide leaded window of the royal bedchamber.

Milli and Bart yawn. They cautiously leave to get dressed.

Ruffy, totally recovered from the venom, pads along behind them.

Cautiously open-eyed, Sharoo and Clyde meditate.

Deep breathing helps them feel better. They attain a fragile state of peace.

After a while, they stretch and whisper to their Floaters.

"Morning, Eedoo."

"Morning, Eeroo."

Simultaneously, the Floaters reply. Their words sound in Clyde's head as well as in Sharoo's.

You may now be told something about the recent intruder.

The creature that attacked Ruffy had the ability to "fade" itself, to blend almost perfectly with the background. Its name, translated, would be "Blender." Except for a slight shimmer or shine, Blenders are totally invisible. They stick to walls, watching and waiting. At a time of their choosing, they sedate their victims and leisurely ingest them.

Sharoo gasps. "That Blender was with us, watching! We kept *almost* seeing it! Hey, why did it blink off and on?"

In its greed, the Blender became partially visible as it prepared to eat Ruffy. It had decided that the dog would be the tastiest.

"Ugh!" Sharoo turns to Clyde. "Thank the O.B.E. you blasted it!"

"Yeah, Roo. But there's still another Blender on the loose!"

Sharoo tilts back her head. "What should we do?" Her voice is shaky. "How can we stop the other Blender . . . if it stays blended?"

The two Floaters again reply as one. *Remain alert. Blenders are highly intelligent, but vicious and ruthless. They can move very fast.*

"How can we find the other one?" Clyde whispers. "We can't let it go around paralyzing people and . . ." His words trail away.

There is no reply.

At morn-meal, Sharoo and Clyde tell Milli and Bart what their Floaters said. Vicious, ruthless Blenders!

Milli shudders. "Now what? Will the other Blender drop down from the ceiling on top of somebody?" She reaches down to hug Ruffy.

Bart is too shocked to joke. "What are we supposed to do?" he asks.

"Stay alert," Sharoo tells him. "Blenders can move very fast. I'll ask Inspector Columbo to give everyone in the castle a pistol."

"What about the citizens?" asks Milli.

"We can't give them guns without causing a panic," Clyde tells her. "Many might die."

"Where's Charlton?" asks Bart. "I'm dying of hunger!"

As if on cue, Charlton enters to announce that Chef Soofull has created a special morn-meal, a marvelous surprise.

"Bring it on," says Clyde. "We're famished."

"Yes, Your Majesty." The Chief Steward bows, hiding a grin.

Soon he carries in a silver tray with four blue porcelain plates. A foot or so *above each plate* hovers a square, golden-brown pastry!

Milli stares. "What . . . are those?"

Charlton smiles. "Chef Soofull calls them Wafting Waffles, Duchess."

"What's in them?" Sharoo asks.

"He refuses to say, Your Majesty. But two wizards paid him a visit last night." Charlton winks knowingly. "This morning I saw him mixing scruffbird eggs, flour, spiced oatmeal, snood-paste, and two thin powders in a large bowl. I'm certain it's the wizards' ingredients that make them fly."

Clyde looks suspicious. "Maybe I'll order him to tell us."

The hovering waffles drop to the plates.

"You deflated them," says Bart. "Waffles have their pride."

Sharoo smiles. "Well, we won't spoil Chef Soofull's secret."

The waffles happily rise again.

Charlton smothers a laugh.

The four teenagers attempt to butter their Waffles in mid-air. As they press down, the sugary pastries sink, then bob back up again.

Milli stares. "It's sort of creepy, the way they float back up. I keep thinking they're alive."

"You can't keep a good waffle down," says Bart with a grin.

"Yuck!" Milli drops her butter knife, clutches her stomach. "Don't say that!"

Sharoo queasily gulps.

"Pardon, Highness." Charlton leans forward. "Chef Soofull asked me to inform you that the waffles should rest comfortably, inside, until fully digested."

"But what if they don't?" asks Clyde.

"Who's afraid of a little dough?" says Bart. "I'm starved!"

Grabbing his waffle with both hands, he bravely takes a bite. His eyes light up. "Yum!"

The others cautiously follow his example. The waffles are delicious.

Carpenters arrive to replace Milli's broken door.

The four royal teenagers nervously watch. When will the other Blender appear? Will they be able to see it, if it does?

All day they start at the slightest sound, at every play of sunlight, every subtle reflection . . . Is it the other Blender, or their imaginations?

Auff drops a dish in the pantry. Everyone jumps.

The teletalker chimes. They jerk like puppets on strings.

"This is intolerable!" Sharoo declares. "I almost wish the other Blender would appear."

"It won't appear," says Clyde. "It *blends*. That's its name."

"You know what I mean," Sharoo tells him. "We're all going crazy with suspense."

"Yeah," says Milli. "It's driving me mangos!" She muses for a moment. "Maybe the other one didn't get through before Mrs. Zaura closed the portals."

"Eedoo is never wrong," Sharoo declares.

No one argues.

"At least there won't be any more Loopers," says Bart. "You burned their britches behind them."

Milli giggles.

Sharoo nervously laughs.

That night, guards are posted everywhere. Everyone locks their doors, but they can't sleep. The first Blender smashed Milli's door, so no one is safe!

Everyone sleeps with a pistol.

Clyde keeps the Looper ray-gun on his bedside table.

His troubled dreams are interrupted by a high-pitched, terrified scream.

"Milli! Open up! It's me, Clyde." He hears muffled dog-whimpers.

"Sorry, Clyde. Ruffy heard a noise in the heating pipes. He went berserk. He remembers that awful Blender."

No more sleep for anyone.

Three days anxiously pass.

On a sunny Tenday morning, the four sleepy teenagers go to the temple meditation-and-prayer service. Amazingly, the Blenders remain a secret outside of the castle. Even Awn and Auff haven't blabbed.

Mother Maura bows and greets them with a reverent "mastie," her hands pressed flat together to form a little mast. They bow and greet her in return. Clyde has the ray-gun under his shirt; the others pack hidden pistols.

During the service, they feel safer, sitting on palm-frond prayer mats among the meditating people. They pray to the O.B.E. for the Blender to be captured and destroyed.

Two nervous days later, on a rainy Twoday morning, a lone dolphin cloud performs joyous somersaults above the castle. Huge raindrops shatter like transparent marbles on the castle's craggy roof.

Morn-meal, as usual, is tense. The four teenagers are groggy with sleep deprivation. Will the other Blender attack today?

Charlton enters the dining hall and bows.

"Pardon, Your Majesties. Awn and Auff have exciting news to report. They will tell it only to you. May I admit them?"

"Why not?" says Clyde.

The two lads enter and bow. "Your Majesties!" says Auff, tossing back his long green hair. "We found this really weird skeleton."

"Where?" asks Sharoo.

Awn picks his acne. "Behind the castle, Highness. Below a boa vine. We think it might be the other Blender. You can see all the bones."

The four royal teenagers jump up from the table.

"Show us!" cries Clyde.

Sure enough, beneath a maypole tree, the Blender's eerie skull stares hollowly up at the snaky green vine that ensnared it.

Four cheers shatter the still morning air.

Sharoo gives Awn and Auff each a bottle of special reserve mango brandy. Then she regrets it. Then she's glad she did.

Broan city's best scientists spend several days marveling at the strange jumble of visible rubbery bones. The Blender's venom has evaporated.

Still, the boa vine withers and dies.

EIGHTEEN

How do plashlings perceive the passage of Time? Much like earthlings. For the very young, Time resembles a puffy cloud, lazily resting overhead. Its imperceptible progress is frustrating. "How soon is my birfday, Mama?"

Later in life, Time moves faster, like a bird steadily flapping across the sky. People are often too busy to notice. "Time flies," they might observe.

For the very old, Time zooms through the air like an arrow, shot from a powerful bow. It whizzes past almost before you know it. "Why, I'm old!"

On Plash, ten years have steadily passed.

The Queen and King of Broan have been married for more than ten years!

Already they have two children: Prince Boldi, almost four, and Princess Pleezi, barely two. Boldi has Clyde's dark, curly hair. Pleezi has Sharoo's silky yellow hair and Clyde's delicate emerald eyes.

Duchess Milli and Duke Bart have twin girls! Their marriage was also a splendid affair. In her flowery dress, Milli looked like a beautiful peacock.

Pudgy Bart has now become a strikingly handsome young man! He works out regularly in one of the castle's old dungeons.

Late one afternoon, the King and Queen sip drinks on the flagstone terrace. Clyde seems dreamy and far away.

"A flutterby for your thoughts," Sharoo teases.

"Wha— Oh, yeah. It just occurred to me, Roo. Broan is primitive. We need progress. Scientific advancement. Like those Looper ray-guns."

Sharoo nods. "But we're safe now. The portals are closed."

"Yes. But aliens from our own universe might pay us a visit. And not a friendly one." He pauses to let her imagine this. "We need to be able to protect Broan. Besides, this country is backward. Our citizens could use a few modern conveniences."

Sharoo's eyes are wide. "You're right." She thinks for a moment. "Hey! Remember those Wafting Waffles? Chef Soofull used Wizard magic! What if our scientists did the same thing?"

Clyde springs from his throne. "Great idea! We'll have mountains of fantastic progress!"

Three leading scientists and three famous magickers are summoned to the castle. Three men and three women. A lot of white hair, wrinkles, and beards.

"You are The Chosen Six," says the King, "You must work together."

The magickers grumble among themselves, mentioning spells and charms that the Queen and King have never heard of.

Lionizis, a wrinkled old witch with white hair, steps forward. "Your Majesties! Broan is indeed, as you put it, somewhat lacking in scientific advancement." She solemnly fingers her chin. "But are the people morally prepared?" Her eyes glow red beneath tangled white brows. "Are they spiritually advanced enough . . . to handle magical science properly?"

The King and Queen hastily assure Lionizis that they are.

The old woman's snowy eyebrows rise. She confers with the other magickers, who grumble and nod.

"Very well, Your Majesties," Lionizis croaks. "It shall be so!"

The Chosen Six bow and depart.

Sharoo briefly recalls what Eedoo said about earthlings: "Their moral progress has lagged behind their scientific achievements." But she quickly shrugs it away. Magical science will be so exciting!

The Chosen Six form a secret organization called the F.B.I. (Foremost Bureau of Inventions). They begin work at once . . .

Progress hatches like a giant dragon's egg! Broanians soon have color Televiewers with magicksound.

Wonderful medicines abound! Of course, advertising shamelessly proliferates. One day Prince Boldi, who watches a lot of TV, tells Sharoo: "Mama, I have a moderate to severe tummy ache."

Each citizen has a FingerFone! Personal history is stored in The Sky.

Horse-drawn carriages are extinct. People drive sleek automotors.

Kids zoom everywhere on M.P.R.s (magick-powered rollerboards).

There is also a new drink called snoffee, made from fermented snoods. The steaming yellow liquid produces a two-hour jolt of bracing energy, but it causes people to act rashly.

Thanks to the F.B.I., the children of Broan have amazing toys.

Swinging, brightly-colored mobiles play peek-a-boo above

Boldi's bed and Pleezi's crib. Singing soapcakes swim circles in their golden bath.

Unfortunately, Prince Boldi grows naughty. He is stubborn and spoiled. Sharoo doesn't believe in "switching" as some parents do. She recalls with horror the Zapper that Mr. Sade employed years ago at school.

What should she do? She asks Eedoo. Her Floater doesn't answer, but soon an idea strikes her. When Boldi misbehaves, he must sit in a green leather chair. "I'm so sorry!" she tells the boy. "You must sit there for fifteen minutes. There is nothing I can do."

Little Boldi accepts this. The green chair takes the Ego out of disciplining! There is no "*I* told you . . ." Sharoo is now on the Prince's side, helping him to cope with the implacable green chair!

On Boldi's fifth birthday, a bald scientist called Snuff (one of The Chosen Six) arrives at the castle with a bulging beige bag.

The Prince looks cute in his blue seaman's suit.

Snuff bows before the Queen. He pulls a brown bear from his bag and, with a flourish, places it on the floor before the boy.

Prince Boldi squints. The smiling bear sits dumbly on its fuzzy butt.

"See? It meditates!"

"Uh-huh." Boldi yawns.

Suddenly, the bear rises up in the air!

Boldi gapes. "Mama, look!"

Sharoo stares. "It's levitating!" she exclaims.

Boldi's eyes are huge. "Mama, if I meditate, will I . . . lefikate?"

Sharoo smiles. "Maybe something *even better* will happen."

"Oh, goodie-wow!" He makes a quick little mastie.

Sharoo enthusiastically thanks the scientist.

"My pleasure, Your Highness. It was fun to create the Levitating Meditating Teddy." Snuff returns to his beige bag. "And now, the Boom Ball!" He holds out a golden kickball, with streaks of silver lightning on the side.

Boldi covers his ears with both hands.

Snuff laughs. "No, my dear Prince. The Boom is for boomerang, not noise." He bows to Sharoo. "It's perfect for teaching the L.O.B."

The bald man taps the ball smartly with his foot. It rolls across the room, stops abruptly, and returns.

"Cool!" Prince Boldi chortles with joy. "Can I do it?"

"Yes, dear," Sharoo tells him. "You *may*."

Boldi gives the Boom Ball a solid kick, and it performs well.

The scientist grins. "The bear and the ball are a bit pricey, Highness. But not for you, of course. A hundred gold crowns will suffice."

"Hmm," says Sharoo.

"And last but not least," Snuff hurriedly continues, "Mocko-Choco!" He brandishes a tall, dark bottle. "This magic sauce makes vegetables taste like chocolate. It makes *anything* taste like chocolate! Even nasty cough medicine. The royal children will beg for it, Your Highness."

Sharoo's eyes light up. "Oh, thank you! They always spit the cough medicine out."

When the scientist departs, his beige bag tinkles and clinks.

Boldi meditates seriously now. Little Pleezi tries it too.

Duchess Milli and Duke Bart are also inspired to meditate more. After a few weeks, they seem close to finding their Floaters!

"I think I could do it," Milli announces one day at mid-meal. "But living in this luxurious castle inflates my Ego."

Bart nods. "There's an old joke," he says. "A circus needs a lion-tamer. Two people apply for the job: a grubby old man and a beautiful young lady in a raincoat." He smirks. "The lady enters the lion cage, slips off the raincoat, and she's stark naked! The ferocious lion whimpers like a kitten, licks her feet, licks her legs, higher and higher . . . The old man's eyes are like saucers.

"The circus director turns to the man. 'What can you do to compare with that?'"

"'Get that lion out of there,' says the man, 'and I'll do my best!'"

Clyde laughs.

"Well," says Bart, "when I meditated this morning, I suddenly thought: 'Get that Ego out of there, and I'll do my best!'"

NINETEEN

Ruffy is old. The curly black sheephound goes gray around the snout. After a few months, his legs give way. Bart and Clyde take turns carrying him outside.

In the royal limousine, Milli takes Ruffy to the dog doctor, a long-haired, green-skinned young man. After a quick examination, he throws up his hairy, light-green hands. "What can I tell you? This noble hound has already outlived his normal life expectancy. You should be grateful, Duchess. Ruffy is not in pain. Yet." He gives her some little yellow pills. "At the end, these will allay his suffering."

Ruffy knows he is fading away. His puzzled brown eyes plead for help. Milli tries to console him. Then she retires to her bedchamber and sobs.

It hits Clyde hard, too. He has always loved the friendly, goofy dog. Haunted by Ruffy's pleading eyes, he meditates and prays . . .

"Eeroo!" he whispers. "Does this have to happen?"

You know perfectly well that it does. You are a sensitive person. The dog has had a good, happy life. And you saved him from the Blender.

"Yes, but it's still so sad. Is there anything I can do?"

Pray to the O.B.E. for the hound to have a fortunate rebirth.

Clyde does his best.

)) ((

Ruffles is given a royal funeral, ordered by King Clyde. A five-cannon salute. Trumpets blare. The sheephound is more honored than are many respected people!

A few citizens grumble. "All this for a dead dog?" says Eligh Krindle, whose beloved Aunt Wista recently passed away.

"The hound killed a Blender, you ninny!" Marci Farko objects.

"No, he never!"

"Did too. Almost got killed hisself. Anyways, the King and Queen have saved us many times! They can do what they want, with chimes on."

It's eerie! In the dining hall, Milli swears she can hear Ruffy's moist snuffles and plaintive whines. When this happens, Clyde (who can't believe he's doing it) waves a scrap of bacon beneath the table. Nobody laughs.

One evening, after meditation, Clyde tilts back his head. "Eeroo! Is it possible that Ruffy's ghost haunts the castle?"

Yes. His invisible spirit form lingers. The dog is fully conscious, and thinks he is still alive. His spirit will soon fade away and enter a deep sleep. That will end only when Ruffy is reborn as a human boy, a boy who will likely become a gentle pet-store owner later in life.

Clyde tells this to Milli, and it consoles her.

Before long, the Duchess purchases a puppy. A chocolate-brown weenie-hound, with a white streak on her forehead. The frisky pup has golden eyes. Her legs are white, all the way up to her knees.

She's so cute! The twins giggle with glee.

Milli wonders what to name her. Rompy? Weenie? Saucy? Snowy? Nothing completely appeals.

The next morning, Bart says: "Let's call her Man."

Milli's jaw drops. "It's a female, Bart! Anyway, who ever heard of a dog called Man?"

Bart shrugs. "She can be Manny then, with Man for short. Manny of the white socks and golden eyes."

Sharoo smiles. "Why not? It's original."

Bart leans down close to the puppy. "How's it going, Man?"

The weenie-hound barks excitedly. She has a squeaky bark.

Clyde laughs. "She likes it. I like it too."

Bart tries again. "Hey, Man. What's up down there?"

The puppy jumps up and down, barking happily.

"All right," says Milli. "You win. Manny it is."

All is well now, except that the twins can't resist pulling Manny's floppy ears. The puppy squeals—and hides under sofas and chairs.

Bart solves this by firmly pulling the twins' ears. And taking the opportunity to talk about the Law of Boomerang.

One afternoon, Manny vanishes! The puppy simply disappears.

"Let's have a manhunt," says Bart.

Milli groans.

No one in the castle can find Manny. It's almost uncanny.

"Maybe she fell into a manhole."

"It's not funny, Bart. Manny might be hurt."

"Then she'll need a Manny cure," Bart suggests.

"Aargh!" Milli sounds like a pirate. "No more jokes!"

That evening, Charlton unlocks the wine cellar, and Manny scampers out! The puppy had followed the Chief Steward in, and stayed to sniff the fragrant cases of wine.

Now, as Milli hugs her, Manny guiltily whimpers.

"No more whining," says Bart.

TWENTY

Almost unbelievably, fifty more years have passed!

As now-skimpy-white-haired Bart puts it, "Time has been speeding up for some time."

The King and Queen marvel at Time's sneaky acceleration. They are seventy-five already! Both still in good health, thank the O.B.E. Hale and ticking, as Broanians like to say.

Queen Sharoo's silky blonde hair has gone silver. She was starting to feel achy and stiff, but Akhta Yugo keeps her flexible, nimble, and healthy.

Clyde's dark, curly hair, in Bart's words, is now "peppered with salt." He has the start of a double chin, and a loveable little pot belly. Sharoo begs him to exercise like Bart.

"You don't want to become an old duddy-fuddy," she tells him.

"I'm hardly that," he replies. "I could start exercising any day now."

Sharoo sighs. "Any day, as they say, might never come your way."

Little Prince Boldi has long been a handsome man! His elegant pointy "goat beard" is going gray. At fifty-five, he seems an able heir to the throne, followed by Princess Pleezi, fifty-three. Boldi has a lovely wife and little son, but Pleezi never married.

Boldi recently found his Floater, and Pleezi found hers long ago! Their parents always encouraged them to meditate.

Combined with magic, scientific inventions are now miraculous! Amazing medical breakthroughs. Body-part replacements. Mind-games like Chessers.

So much has happened in fifty years! Broanians wear a thin red strip with a silver forehead disk called an eyeBand. This amazing device connects the wearer with the endless information stored in The Sky.

The Queen and King have totally forgotten the wise words of Lionizis: "But are they morally ready?" They are unaware that for many years The Chosen Six (four already replaced) have secretly *decreased* their input of magic.

Why? Many Broanians are devious and corrupt. The boon of scientific advancement has partially backfired. People have devised innovative ways to cheat and steal. But there are no ray-guns. Only accurate, five-shot pistols. Sharoo insisted on that.

Even so, young children are now exposed to violence, bloodshed, and sex, both on TV and on their FingerFones.

Concerned about corruption and graft, the Queen and King decree that all citizens must meditate daily. Additional bamboo temples are built. Teachers are trained. A few dedicated meditators connect with their Floaters!

Sharoo and Clyde spend time sitting on their thrones, reminiscing.

"Hey, Roo," says Clyde, fingering his fleshy chin. "Remember how little Boldi used to love that actionmag *Scarytales*? He couldn't wait to watch the next episode of Superclown."

Sharoo nods, smiling. "How could I forget? When Superclown's big red nose tingled, it meant that a crime was being plotted. His sad eyes cried. The tears streaked down his whitewashed cheeks."

"Yeah," says Clyde. "Superclown's floppy shoes had magic air-fins, so he could fly!"

"Right!" Sharoo smiles. "His white gloves were lightning-fast, snatching bullets from the air!"

Clyde gazes dreamily into space. "Little Boldi used to sing: Look! Up in the sky! It's a rainbow! A rocket! It's Superclown!"

Sharoo's misty gaze is far away. "We gave Pleezi a Story-telling Doll and a bottle of perfume for her fifth birthday, remember? We told her it was impolite to brag. She went around saying: "If you hear a little noise and smell a little smell, it's me!""

Clyde laughs, remembering.

The ancient seer Mrs. Zaura is *still* alive and cackling. She still occupies her cozy guest room in the castle. There are rumors that she is five hundred years old (half a go-on!) and drinks the blood of a newborn gazoo at midnight. Actually, the old woman imbibes a thick potion made from finely ground herbs and pickled snoods. Plus a few drops of witchy youth-elixir.

King Klauzer of Blore recently sent a telemail in which he apologized for the Morfers' past behavior. They are ashamed of abducting Broanians in order to fatten and ingest them. It was unspeakably barbaric! On behalf of all his citizens, the King sincerely regrets the invasion. Morfers now eat an artificial substance called Beyondflesh . . .

Sharoo sighs. Should she believe this? She recalls how, so long ago, she thought up a magic spell that allegedly protected Plash from evil invaders. The spell supposedly made invaders go insane. She smiles. The roach-like Morfers were fooled, but do they now suspect the truth? Do they still eat living beings? Do they "hunger" for revenge? Will Broan's defenses prove adequate? She wonders, uneasily.

In his old age, Clyde has become forgetful. Sharoo persuades him to take powdered snoods that Mrs. Zaura mixes with other herbs to ward off senility.

Alas! Clyde contracts a case of demon-see, a disease that sometimes afflicts older Broanians. He begins to see impish demons. Elusive phantoms. Mysterious faces shimmer in glass-covered pictures, mirrors, and windowpanes. He is ashamed to tell Sharoo. He knows the disease is fatal.

It gets worse. Clyde writhes in fear. He clamps his eyes shut, but demons pursue him *even through his eyelids.*

No longer can he fool Sharoo.

The King sits trembling on his throne. He grows weaker every day.

Sharoo implores Eedoo: "What can I do?"

The answer shakes her. *Pray. In a distant-past life, Clyde was a hunter who took pleasure in . . . things you would not wish to hear about. But he has a good chance to become a skillful surgeon in his next incarnation.*

The evil demons attack in droves! They dance through Clyde's head, assuming terrible glowing shapes. Are they spirits? Ghosts? Ghasts?

Modern science, though enhanced by magic, is helpless. Doctors come, examine the King, and sadly shake their heads.

Sharoo is heartbroken. She is slowly, cruelly losing Clyde, a little every day. But she loves him just as much, perhaps even more! Even now, he is so *precious*. Warm tears slide down her cheeks when she's alone.

Clyde slowly passes away, holding Sharoo's hand and whispering to his Floater Eeroo. He dies much more peacefully than last time, when Blizza stabbed him.

Sharoo gives the King a grand funeral. Wrinkled Milli sobs. Bart freely weeps. Charlton, who was replaced by his grandson Bates, died long ago.

Realizing how fragile life is, Sharoo invents a new acronym: O.A.R. "May I make the best use of my opportunities, abilities, and resources."

In King Clyde's memory, the Queen establishes several charitable organizations. She orders still more bamboo temples built. Father Frendzi (who replaced Mother Maura when she passed away) goes from one temple to another, leading prayer and meditation services.

The Queen is now called "Sharoo the Wise."

Sharoo vividly recalls her deceased mother, Ida Loo. Before bed, her mama always read to her from *Dotti in the Land of Odd*. It was giggle-out-loud funny, but scary too. Little Dotti and her dog Zozo are swallowed by a sinkhole! Lost in a weird, underground world, they struggle to find their way home . . .

Dotti meets a kind-hearted tinman, a wise, talking crow, and a roaring, ticklish lion. Together, they go on a dangerous quest to find The Diamond City. Why? It is ruled by The Wizard of Odd.

Maybe he will grant their wishes! By chance, Dotti discovers that The Great Odd is cheating his worker-gnomes. When she threatens to expose him, Odd uses his magic to send her home.

The aging Queen also recalls her papa, Wyfur Loo. At first, he didn't believe in Eedoo, and after he took a swipe at her Floater, he had a serious accident at the lumber mill. She remembers how her papa secretly poured rye whiskey into his morning coffee. Thank the O.B.E. she helped him to control his addiction!

Her papa read her only one story, but he read it many times. It was called "The Girl Who Cried Foon." A little girl loved to pretend she had seen a rare foon. "Foon! Foon!" she would cry, whereupon the villagers rushed out with big sacks to capture the valuable animal. The little girl secretly giggled to see such a frantic fuss. She knew it was wrong to lie, but couldn't help it.

One day, an old wizard watched this from his tower "with burning eyes." All of a sudden, in a puff of green smoke, the little girl was transformed into a shaggy brown foon! As she slowly understood what had happened, "she sniffed with her whiskered nose, and her almond eyes filled with tears." Little Sharoo always shuddered at those words.

Where are her mama and papa now? In her aging memory, they seem suspiciously vivid! Are they aware that she is thinking about them? If so, can they send a signal from where they are? Or were they reborn long ago?

TWENTY-ONE

One Oneday afternoon, the aging Queen reclines on a purple chaise lounge on the west terrace. Near the castle door, a tall guard named Blake stands watch.

On her FingerFone, Sharoo reads a popular book called *Getting Old Is Getting Old*. The author's main point is that with modern medical science, you're as young as you think you are—but only in the morning.

Sharoo yawns. She looks up. Against the azure-blue sky, the trees are a glorious yellow-gold. A few small birds chirp in red-orange bushes.

Sharoo smiles. The pale autumn sun kisses her face. She puts down her FingerFone, sits erect, and meditates . . .

All of a sudden, she's aware that the birds have ceased their chirping. The castle gardens are strangely hushed. It reminds her of something.

The silence seems strangely alive. Sharoo opens her eyes.

A lovely shape steps out from between two oaks, moving slowly toward her. Sharoo sees a gray-white coat, a soft rainbow shimmer. A pearly horn, a silky gray mane. It's a unicorn!

Can it be . . . Poppi? Sharoo recalls the time, so long ago, when she met this beautiful animal in the forest, near Mrs. Zaura's little hut. Can it really be the same unicorn? How long do they live? And why—

Across the terrace, beside the castle wall, Blake raises his high-powered pistol. He looks questioningly at the Queen.

"No!" Sharoo strongly mouths the word. "No!" She pulls down her flattened palm. The guard understands, lowers his weapon.

Poppi's hooves clomp gently on the flagstones. She steadily approaches the sitting Queen.

Sharoo waits in awe. From the distant past, Mrs. Zaura's words echo in her head: *It's good luck to see her.*

The beautiful creature reaches the Queen, bends down her gentle face. The unicorn's luminous eyes are expressive, like Clyde's.

Sharoo shyly reaches out her wrinkled hand. She strokes the smooth, warm head, touches the twisty horn. A vibrant energy travels up her arm in its purple velvet sleeve.

Poppi nods. Her mouth forms a barely perceptible smile. She slowly turns away, clomps back to the forest edge, and disappears.

The next day, at morn-meal, Prince Boldi says: "Mama, wouldn't it be safer to do this over the televiewer?"

"Yes," Princess Pleezi agrees. "There's a lot of unrest in the city."

"No," says the Queen. "I want to be close to my people."

Her two children exchange worried glances.

"As you wish, Mama," says Boldi.

An hour later, the silver-haired Queen addresses a huge crowd in Palisades Park. She stands on a small platform before a golden microphone, stamped with the black letters Q.S. She looks dignified in her flowing yellow robes.

Sharoo takes slow, deep breaths. This is an important speech. The clear, sunlit air is cold and crisp.

A horde of expectant faces gaze at their beloved Queen.

"Citizens of Broan!" Sharoo's voice is husky but strong. She clears her throat. "Your Queen will soon step down from the throne. It is time to turn it over to my son, Prince Boldi. He has found his Floater, and is well prepared to—"

Whisst! A sound like a hissing viper-snake cuts the air.

Queen Sharoo staggers slightly. On her chest, a shocking red flower blossoms. *Whisst!* A second shot strikes her as well.

Too late, mounted detectors identify the weapon, which was cloaked by purple magic. Powerful neutralizing rays freeze the assassin.

Medical attendants rush to the wounded Queen. They surround her, applying medical devices . . .

A medicopter lands beside them. The door swishes open.

Guards hold back the moaning, murmuring crowd.

Sharoo is flown to morbacare.

The ray-frozen assassin, it soon develops, is a man named Zlodi Trillbar. He is a trippie, the son of Fardoo, whose father was the thug who killed Queen Reeya and King Kilgore. When Zlodi fired his cloaked weapon, he was jacked on rotweed and snoffee. He was filled with visions of revenge, convinced by distorted family lore that Queen Sharoo ordered his grandfather tortured. Actually, she had mostly showed mercy on the killer.

The Queen of Broan lies in a white morbacare bed, surrounded by male and female doctors.

They confer in subdued voices.

From the few words she can hear, Sharoo concludes that her condition is hopeless.

"Eedoo!" she whispers. "Am I dying?"

Yes.

"Can they do anything to keep me alive?"

No.

"Doctor!" the Queen calls to the nearest woman in white. "I wish to die in my castle."

The doctor nods gravely. "Yes, Your Highness."

Prince Bondi provisionally assumes the crown.

Does the Queen fear death? No, it is time.

In her cozy guest room, Mrs. Zaura trances beside her quarzz crystal and waxlight. A tear rolls down her wrinkled cheek.

Wounds carefully bandaged, Sharoo lies in her royal bed. She's propped up by two soft pillows. A searing sharpness burns her chest. Another bullet-hole burns in her side.

The pain is exhausting. Her tortured body goes limp. She weakly groans.

For the third time, a tall man in white offers her drugs for the pain. She shakes her head. "No, doctor, thank you. I want to keep my mind clear, so I can meditate . . . and keep in touch with my Floater."

The doctor rolls his eyes. "As you wish, Highness."

Sharoo lies quietly, meditating the best she can. She is about to cry out when she flashes on something Eedoo once told her. *Maybe you should think about someone else.*

Sharoo prays to the O.B.E. for Clyde's spirit to be well. And for Boldi and Pleezi to have fulfilled, healthy lives. But the pain still burns. There's an old Broanian proverb: "Your own pain hurts worse."

Then she has an inspiration.

Sharoo improvises a prayer. "May my pain help as many beings as possible not to suffer." She repeats this over and over. The burning diminishes.

In her head, Eedoo's words sound softly. *Well prayed. You will soon find peace.*

It is dark. Only a sliver of moon. A unicorn, head bowed, appears beside the castle. Poppi rubs her rainbow horn gently against the jeweled wall.

In her royal bedchamber, the dying Queen flinches. She has a faint sense of recognition. Does she imagine that Poppi has come to bid her farewell?

"Thank you, Eedoo," she whispers. "For all your wonderful help. Thank you, O.B.E., for letting me have such a fortunate life."

At the moment of death, Sharoo feels her consciousness pass from her flesh body *into another plane of existence.*

Eedoo welcomes her, quietly and lovingly.

TWENTY-TWO

On another plane of existence, Sharoo opens her nonphysical eyes. Her mental eyes. She is fully, but differently, conscious.

Her mind senses a nearby Presence: radiant, coldly analytical, loving.

"Where am I?"

Not a place. A state of being.

"What does that mean?"

You are no longer Sharoo. You are the you you always were.

"What should I do?"

Not do. Recall, evaluate, learn. We have done this before.

Her mental eyes widen. She has a vision of a snowy-haired wizard, lying on a small, rumpled bed.

"I . . . was Wombler!"

Yes.

"And after I died as Wombler, I learned . . . not to be so proud. To overcome my Ego, as I put it."

Yes. And before that, you were Queen Quist.

She mentally gasps. She sees a yellow face with bright red hair, wearing a crown like hers. Queen Quist was a Silver Dragon too. "Puffed up with pride, the great Quist died," people say.

Right. Great abilities are a two-edged blade. Queen Quist was arrogant, self-kissed. Wizard Wombler, somewhat less. What were the high points of your life as Sharoo?

The former Queen thinks back. Her memory is now so strong, so clear! "First, I learned about the O.B.E. from my parents. From Mother Maura, in the temple, I learned how to meditate. That, and trying to be good, enabled me to be in touch with my Floater. Hey, where is Eedoo?"

You have left the body called Sharoo. The Floater you called Eedoo is still with you.

"Where am I?"

Not where. This is not a where or when. Please go on.

"Eedoo taught me the Law of Boomerang. Sooner or later, you get what you give. Good or bad. It's automatic."

Yes. Your actions, thoughts, and feelings are like good or bad songs that you sing. Their echoes inexorably return. What else happened?

"Eedoo taught me to meditate more effectively. It soon became a magical, enchanted experience." The former Queen pauses. "I made up the designation A.S.A.P. Alert, Still, And Poised." She smiles.

"And Mrs. Zaura encouraged me to be brave. And a unicorn called Poppi showed me the power of compassion. She did, didn't she?"

Yes. Compassion dissolves Ego.

"I feel like my Ego left together with my body. It's a great relief."

Ego is a sneaky jailer. What else?

"Eedoo taught me about mindmake. The conscious mind creates an idea of the world, based on what the eyes and other senses report. I also learned the difference between mind and brain."

Right. And then?

"Eedoo helped me to control my anger. And to tame my resentment. Clyde taught me to have mercy, when we caught the killer Trillbar. And Eedoo taught me to be grateful for the miraculous gift of consciousness."

What else happened?

"I became overconfident in my star body. Too much Ego."

Yes. What did you learn more recently?

"Too late, I learned that moral advancement should accompany scientific achievements. I tried to make amends, but much remains to be done."

Yes. You have made much spiritual progress. You now have a choice between going to a Permanent Place of Peace . . . or being reborn as a person. Think carefully. This is a big decision.

Sharoo's mind grapples with the choice. She weighs the pros and cons. She thinks of Eedoo, of Clyde, of Mrs. Zaura, of Poppi . . .

There is still so much suffering! She thinks of all the people who die without finding their Floaters.

Mental tears slide down her mental face.

At last, she answers.

"I choose rebirth. If possible, as a person who can help many others.

It shall be so. First, you will have a long, restful sleep. Then you will be reborn, though you will not know it, as a baby girl in the Wombler family. You will call Eedoo "Vizda," and grow up to be a great Wizard-Priestess.